THE DIPLOMATIC
TUTOR

THE DIPLOMATIC TUTOR

•

Sandra Elzie

AVALON BOOKS
NEW YORK

Published by Thomas Bouregy & Co., Inc.
160 Madison Avenue, New York, NY 10016

Library of Congress Cataloging-in-Publication Data

Elzie, Sandra.
   The diplomatic tutor / Sandra Elzie.
      p. cm.
   ISBN 978-0-8034-9973-7 (hardcover : acid-free paper)
   I. Title.
   PS3605.L95D56 2009
   813'.6—dc22

                                        2009012797

PRINTED IN THE UNITED STATES OF AMERICA
ON ACID-FREE PAPER
BY HADDON CRAFTSMEN, BLOOMSBURG, PENNSYLVANIA

To my husband, Richard, the love of my life,
my best friend and my biggest cheerleader.

Chapter One

Natalie Holmes was at her twenty-ninth birthday party, dancing with a ruggedly handsome man in blue jeans and a plaid work shirt, when the call came offering her a position she had trained and prayed for. It was a dream come true, an offer she couldn't refuse. It was the best birthday present she had ever received.

It only took her thirty seconds to weigh the pros and cons and come to a decision. Even having to relocate to the suburbs of New York City wasn't enough to dissuade her from the opportunity of a plum position as tutor to the five-year-old daughter of the British diplomat to the United Nations.

After she tucked her cell phone back in the pocket of her favorite jeans—the faded, butt-hugging denims that had been with her through most of her college years—she danced until the wee hours of the morning. She was no longer celebrating her birthday; she was celebrating a new beginning. When she fell into bed at three AM, there was still a smile on her face.

Over the next two weeks, the mandatory investigation and background check of her family, friends and, of course, her personally, was completed. With only one obstacle standing between her and the position, she had completed the required briefing five days ago on United Nations' protocol and then signed the one-year agreement. Her one suitcase was now packed with all the good clothes she owned and, despite the butterflies fluttering constantly in her stomach, she was ready for the adventure to begin.

The last couple days had been spent moving her things into storage and saying good-bye to her friends. She had heard more words of caution than when she took her first solo drive in her mom's beat-up Chevy, but she refused to allow their discouragement to penetrate the euphoric rose-colored haze that she was looking through.

The much-anticipated day was finally here and she could hardly contain the excitement that robbed her of an appetite and left her stomach churning with nerves.

The plane taxied toward the terminal, and people were gathering their carry-on items in readiness to charge the exits as soon as the gangway was attached and the door was opened. She had flown only once in her life, so she was thankful the flight had been uneventful and, although short, it had been very pleasant.

Natalie was unable to keep the smile off her face when she considered what it would take to put her in a bad mood on this special day. The only things she could think of were drastic or deadly. Only missing the flight or the plane crashing would have been able to ruin the day she had worked for all her life.

When she emerged from the concourse, turning to the right toward baggage claim as the overhead sign directed, she was surprised yet delighted to see the promised driver holding up a card with her name written in bold letters.

"How cool." The words slipped out in a whisper as she headed toward the quaint little man in the black suit. He even carried a black chauffeur's hat and bowed slightly as she approached. Her friends back home would never believe this. Her cell phone was too old to have a built-in camera, so they would just have to take her word for it.

"Hi, I'm Natalie," she smiled.

"Ah, Miss Natalie. It is my pleasure to meet you. My name is Andrew Drummond. Please call me Andrew," he told her, his thin lips spreading to a curved line across the bottom of his pleasant face.

"Would you care to come with me and I'll get your bags?" He respectfully walked alongside her, reaching over to take her briefcase. "I hope you had a good flight?"

By the time the bags arrived and had been loaded into the trunk of the limousine, she and Andrew were good friends. He was jovial, although very proper, putting her at ease immediately.

Sitting in the back of the limousine by herself, her eyes darted around, wanting to memorize every detail so that she could write her mother and tell her how exciting her arrival in New York had been. For the first time in her life, she felt like Cinderella going to the ball. She sent up a quick prayer that her clock wouldn't strike midnight any time soon.

She was a long way from her childhood home in Clendenin, West Virginia, where her family still lived in the house her grandfather had built for his bride seventy years earlier. After her father had died in a coalmine explosion when she was nine years old, her mother had been forced to move back to her parents' home with Natalie and her three brothers.

Natalie was the youngest of the four children, but the only one to go to college. From an early age she had decided that the only way to get off The Hill, as she called the homestead, was to get an education and leave the small town where she had been raised.

She wanted to find a good-paying job in the big city and her chance was finally here. Sheer determination and hard work had gotten her through the university in Charleston, West Virginia, and the recommendation of the dean had allowed her to apply and eventually get her name on the list of approved private teachers used by the delegates at the United Nations.

Today, in her estimation, she had risen to the top of

her profession. She had achieved her goal. She was sitting in a pearl-white limousine, listening to soft music, and watching the passing countryside just like in the movies that had been her passion when she was growing up. Through the movies her imagination had taken her to foreign countries, to the top of the Empire State Building, and into the arms of handsome leading men. Well, she wasn't sure about the foreign lands or the handsome leading man, but she had arrived in New York where she would be able to experience the Empire State Building first hand. Life was good.

She smiled as she remembered a conversation she had overheard between her mother and her grandfather years earlier. They had been discussing their fears that she would want to head west to Hollywood to be an actress. They had been concerned she would want to be in the movies like the ones she loved so much. Her mother had called her a romantic.

No, being an actress had never been her dream. Movies were only an escape to show her the way other people lived. They had helped her formulate her dream of a better life.

"Yes," she admitted softly, staring out the window at the passing trees. "I'm a romantic, and I'm sure there's a prince out there for me, but he'll just have to wait." She had work to do and it was going to take all of her concentration and talent.

Not wanting to miss a thing, she leaned closer to the window, her nose almost touching the glass as her eyes took in all the beauty, concentrating to remember every detail until that evening when she could write it all down in her journal.

Even though she was loved as the youngest child and only girl, her family had never believed in her dreams of a bigger and better life. Despite their teasing and laughter, she had never stopped believing in herself.

"Nattie," her mother had told her, "when you grow up you'll marry some nice boy and have some kids. Get your head out of the clouds, child." Natalie remembered crying herself to sleep that night, wanting desperately for her mother to have faith in her.

Well, regardless of her family telling her that she would never amount to much since she spent too much time with her head in the clouds instead of just accepting who she was and where she had come from, she was thrilled to have finally arrived. She was on her way and nothing could stop her now.

She didn't think she was expecting too much. Life was what you made it. Still she couldn't stop the moment of apprehension or the little bit of good old-fashioned fear that was gripping her stomach like a fist squeezing juice from a grape.

With renewed resolve, she squared her shoulders and relaxed back into the seat. Ten feet from the finish line wasn't the time to stop running or to start thinking about sore muscles. No, it was the time to give it a last kick of effort and cross the finish line with your head up and a smile on your face.

When the gleaming white car rounded a curve in the long sweeping, tree-lined driveway to reveal a stone structure reaching thirty feet toward the bluest sky Natalie had ever seen, her jaw dropped and her hand went up to touch the warm glass that separated her from the beauty spread out in front of her. The grandeur was like nothing she had ever seen except in movies or magazines. It was amazing to think that people really lived like this. She had a difficult time imagining how it would feel to wake up each morning and gaze out on such manicured beauty, but she was thrilled that she was about to find out.

The majestic home was sitting atop a small hill, surrounded by acres and acres of professionally landscaped lawns that were edged by gardens and shrubs that swept down toward groves of trees, standing like sentinels to block the home from the prying eyes of the public.

"Oh my goodness," she breathed, pushing on the button to lower the window. The driver slowed to a stop, giving her a few moments to take in the estate and gather her thoughts.

The window between the driver and the passenger area slid down silently while the driver watched her reaction in the rearview mirror. It was the same with almost everyone he brought to the estate. When leaving the city, people expected trees and grassy fields, but the estate was so much more. It was like a park that invited people to come and enjoy the tranquility. It pleased him that the new tutor appreciated nature and all its beauty.

He was surprised that his employer had hired such a young nanny, by far the youngest yet, but he loved her naive innocence. She took great pleasure in the simple things around her, obviously not accustomed to the benefits that money could buy. When he had first seen her responding to the sign he held up at the airport, he had feared for a few minutes that she might be more interested in Mr. Lancaster versus the child. But it was stars he saw in her eyes, not dollar signs. This whole experience was a new adventure, and he was to be her guide on the trip.

"Well, Miss, what do you think of our humble home?"

Natalie couldn't stop the smile that splashed across her face, reaching her eyes to add a dash of sparkle.

"Wow," she breathed out softly. "This is quite a sight. The only thing missing is a few horses grazing on that lawn over on those slopes down from the house." She grinned at him in the mirror, shaking her head in wonder. "This is utterly fantastic. Does he live here all year?"

"Yes, Miss. He makes the occasional trip back to England, but otherwise, he's here full time."

"Well, I can't blame him. It's truly the most beautiful house and property I have ever seen." West Virginia was green and beautiful, but it was a rustic sort of beauty. This property had blended trimmed lawns and plants with the best features of nature for an awe-inspiring view.

She loved the ivy that surrounded the bottom level of the house on one side, trying to leach its way up the stones. She wondered how many gardeners the estate employed in order to keep the grounds so immaculate.

"Well, Miss, it might interest you to know that there is a stable in the back that houses two Arabian and two Morgan. I think you will find any one of them to be very suitable for riding if you are so inclined."

"Really?" She couldn't believe it. All this and horses too. "Well, you don't have to worry about me ever riding one of them. I've never been on a horse and I'm afraid I'm a little too old to start now. I'd probably break my neck," she laughed. "Just between you and me, I'm a little afraid of horses. They're so big and so strong that I don't think I could ever control one, and if I can't control it, then I don't want to be on it," she admitted sheepishly. Turning back to the window, she sighed. "This place must be absolutely beautiful in the winter when it snows."

"Oh yes. It looks like a Christmas card, for sure." His face relaxed as he watched her. She had hair the color of honey, pulled back into a neat bun at the back of her head. Tiny wisps of hair had escaped to outline her face and partially hide the small gold hoops that adorned her delicate ears. Yes, she was a beauty, but too young. It was really too bad since his employer needed someone special in his life as much as little Kelsey needed a mother.

The ambassador to the UN and his daughter lived in one of New York's most affluent neighborhoods in a home well-suited to his status, but the driver feared his employer was terribly lonely since the death of his wife. Would the new tutor bring life to the house? Only time would tell. The house needed laughter as much as the ambassador and Miss Kelsey.

"Are you ready to continue, Miss?"

Her eyes connected again with his in the rearview mirror. Natalie liked his kind eyes. They were as blue as a summer sky, nestled between two sets of small lines that fanned out on each side of his eyes, telling of a contented, happy disposition. He was like a grandfather who would sneak you a candy before dinner.

"Yes. Thank you."

The window slid up between them and Natalie leaned back in the seat, closing her eyes to hug the moment to herself before she would have to face the family and meet the child who was to be entrusted to her care.

A slight frown marred her face. She felt sorry for the little girl. She didn't know much about Kelsey other than her age and that she had been in the United States less than a year. Her mother had been killed in a car accident a couple years earlier, so Natalie's job was to be somewhat more than just a tutor. She was also expected to be a companion and nanny to the motherless child. She prayed she hadn't taken on too much. She didn't have much experience with children, and had no experience as a mother.

As the limousine glided toward the magnificent home, Natalie marveled at so much beauty compressed into one spot. It was truly like something out of the movies. The driveway was paved and circled in front of massive front stairs that rivaled the ones leading into Tara in *Gone With the Wind*, one of her favorite novels as a child. Six large columns held up the balcony above and white rocking chairs dotted the porch that extended the entire front of the house, fanning out into an octagon gazebo at one corner before wrapping around to a side entrance.

She could imagine the owner sitting out on that porch in the evening to relax in the breeze that came up from the Hudson River below, rocking gently while sipping a cool drink. Oh yes, she thought, she could easily imagine that scene, even putting herself into one of the chairs to sit beside the man and talk together about their day.

Of course, she hadn't even met Mr. Lancaster, only his secretary, but for some reason she imagined him being kind. After all, he had brought his daughter over from England to live with him when he could have left her there with a nanny.

The small child must feel so lost without her mother; not having someone of her own to cuddle up with or to lavish her with love. Well, she thought, she would do her best to give the little girl the love she was probably missing.

As the car rolled along the driveway, Natalie held her breath. She almost felt she needed to pinch herself to be sure she wasn't in a dream. It all seemed so much like a fairy tale. But this was as real as the fragrance of an unknown flower that wafted through her still-open window.

The home loomed larger as the limousine drew closer, gliding to a stop in front of the massive stone building rising up majestically toward the sky. It had a broad front that stood a commanding three stories high, with a section on each end dropping down to two stories. When she realized her mouth was hanging open she snapped it shut, glancing in the rearview mirror to see if the driver had witnessed her awe-struck reaction to the house. Thankfully he was already stepping out of the car.

Natalie quickly picked up her purse from the seat, turning toward the door as the driver opened it. As she stepped out, her attention was drawn to the three-tiered water fountain where the sun sparkled against the water, filling the huge bowls to overflow into the next until it splashed into the pool at the bottom.

A smile darted across her face. She loved the sound of the water. She thought it brought the sound of a babbling brook to the rural location. It reminded her of Big Sandy Creek that ran out behind her grandfather's house back home. She stood for a moment, closed her eyes, and breathed deep. When she exhaled, a smile splashed across her face as she turned to look at the chauffeur.

"I love the smell of trees and flowers and, and . . . and dirt!" Her laughter rang out across the courtyard toward the front door that now stood open in anticipation of her entrance.

She glanced toward the house to see a maid standing at the front door, glaring at her like she had just tracked muddy prints onto the pristine carpet.

Andrew was smiling when he turned slightly, putting his back toward the front door. "Don't mind her, Miss. She's as sour as green apples, but has a kind heart for the child, so she can't be all bad."

Natalie fell in love with the chauffeur in that instant. She would have kissed his weathered cheek if the maid hadn't been watching. Instead she reached over and touched the back of his hand.

"Don't worry about me. When life knocks me down," she said, lowering her voice to a conspirator's whisper, "I bounce." With a sly wink, she turned and headed up the stairs to face the new path that she had chosen.

"Where is my briefcase?" Trenton lifted the newspaper, then a magazine. "It was right here last night before . . ." He stopped looking to walk to the office door. "Kelsey!" His thundering voice reverberated down the hall, causing one of the maids to flinch and almost drop the bottle of furniture polish.

"Yes, Daddy," came the high-pitched answer just before running feet were heard coming down the hall.

When she arrived at his office door, she came to an abrupt halt several steps away from her father. She looked dubious as she stared up into stormy eyes. Why was he so angry? Was she in trouble?

"Would you care to tell me if you've seen my brief-case?"

The little girl started to fidget, her eyes dropping to look at her white tennis shoes with the Disney princess shoelaces, her hands twisting together. "Well . . . I might have," she evaded.

"You 'might have'? Would you mind taking me to the spot that 'might have' my briefcase?" He managed to keep the stern look in place even though he wanted to laugh. He knew good and well that the child knew exactly where his briefcase was, but he wondered why she had taken it. Kelsey was a source of first times lately. She had recently lost her first tooth, taken her first swimming lesson, and the list was growing. He wondered what today would bring.

"Yes, Daddy," she mumbled, turning to slowly lead him up the stairs to her room.

He didn't have to search far. Sitting on her bed was his briefcase, opened and now holding neatly folded clothes . . . Barbie clothes. He stepped around the silent child and walked to the bed to stare down at the miniature outfits stacked in piles inside the case.

"Would you care to explain this?" He stood with his arms crossed, looking as stern as he could. He hated to have to punish her, but she had to learn that not everything was hers to play with. He had told her before not to bother the things in his office and she had blatantly disobeyed by taking the case. "And where are all the papers that were inside?"

Without saying a word or looking at her father, she pointed one small finger toward her closet. When he turned to see where she was pointing, he saw his papers all over the floor of her closet, some bent and all of them out of order.

"What do you have to say about what you did?"

Silence reigned in the room as she continued to stare at the floor, the toe of her shoe tracing a pattern on the carpet.

"Speak up or your punishment will be double. You know the rules," he reminded her, speaking in a low tone and holding his temper on a short leash.

"Barbie needed a suitcase for her clothes, and I didn't have one," she said, her chin resting against her chest as she slumped, resting most of her weight on her left foot. Her voice was barely above a whisper.

"Go to my room and sit in the brown chair until I come in to talk to you," he said, his words clipped off like an army sergeant giving an order.

Her auburn curls fell forward, hiding her eyes as she silently made her way from the room, turning to head slowly down the hall without a backward glance.

"Um, excuse me, sir," the maid stammered.

He was leaning over the briefcase, but at the sound of his maid, he twisted around to stare at the two women who stood staring at his hands. He glanced down, just as he realized they were looking at all the tiny outfits he was cradling in his large hands.

"Oh," he said, chuckling, as he turned to drop the clothes on the twin bed behind him. He stepped forward, extending his now-empty hand toward Natalie.

Natalie was speechless as she reached out to shake his hand. The moment their fingers touched, she felt a warmth run across her skin, an electrifying, tingling sensation like none she had ever felt. She started to pull her hand back, but it was too late to stop the heat from scampering up her arm, across her chest, and up into her face. Mercy, the man had eyes that would entice even the most-confirmed bachelorette to reconsider.

Embarrassed by her thoughts, her eyes dropped to trail down his suited body. When she realized she was staring at his belt buckle, she jerked her eyes back up to meet his, her face warm and her eyes opening slightly more than normal, as her mind stumbled for something to say to ease the moment.

He was an imposing man, probably early forties, with broad shoulders and a deep voice. Natalie thought he was one of the most handsome men she had ever seen up close. He carried himself with an aristocratic ease and grace that dared anyone to defy him, but she had seen tenderness in his eyes when he looked at his daughter that belied the tough outer shell that he projected.

Her throat was dry as her mind searched for the proper way to address an ambassador. The man standing before her could have been in any Hollywood movie, but he was her boss. She had been silent too long and she could feel the heat rising up her neck. She wished there were a graceful way to turn and run.

If nothing else, her mother had taught her manners. "Good morning, sir. I'm Natalie Holmes, the new tutor," she smiled, a nervous laugh tucked safely just out of reach. The last thing she needed right now was to laugh at her employer just because she and the maid had eavesdropped on him scolding his child and then observed him removing miniature pink outfits from his briefcase.

"It wouldn't do at all to open my case at the office and have evening attire fall out onto my desk, now would it?" When she only shook her head, he continued.

"It's nice to finally meet you, Miss Holmes. I apologize for not being available for the interview, but I totally trust my secretary to hire someone competent."

"Thank you. I'm glad to be here." She tugged again, reluctantly pulling her hand back, but not quite knowing what to do with it now that it was free. Finally she decided to just hold her hands in front of her to be sure she didn't fidget.

She couldn't believe how blue his eyes were as he stared down at her. Although she was considered slender and had practiced until she could walk with style and grace, she still sometimes felt tall and awkward at five feet, seven inches. It was a pleasant surprise that Mr. Lancaster towered over her by nine or ten inches. It made her feel small and feminine. She stood a little taller, squaring her shoulders just as he cleared his throat and stepped back, bumping his legs into the twin bed.

"Good, good. Well, um, I'll be talking with Kelsey about playing with my things, and then I'll be leaving for the office," he said, stepping around her to stop at the closet to gather the papers and stuff them inside the case before snapping it shut and standing again to face her. "I'll expect you to get up to speed with her lessons within the next few days and then give me a report weekly on her progress." He nodded, stepping over the Barbie dollhouse, making it almost out the door when he stopped.

"Is that satisfactory with you?" He asked the question even as he was turning to leave.

He held the briefcase with both hands like a barrier between the two of them that he didn't want removed; a wall that she would have to scale if she planned to get to him. Heaven forbid, she thought.

"Yes, that's satisfactory, but . . ." She stopped in mid-sentence since he had whirled and was already halfway down the hall.

"Well, that settles that," the maid quipped.

Natalie had forgotten about the maid until she spoke. She was now standing to the side of the room with a slight smile, like a spectator who had just enjoyed a good show. Natalie wanted to wipe the smirk off the woman's lips, but decorum didn't allow for women brawling in the house. Her mother had always told her and her brothers to take their fights outside. Well, she was willing. At least she knew early on who was a friend and whom she would have to keep an eye on.

With her head held high, she turned to face the maid.

"Could you please show me to my room?"

"Certainly." The little smile disappeared as she stepped back into her role as a maid. "Come this way," she instructed, stepping from the room into a long hall that had several doors leading off from it on both sides.

"This is your room, right next to Miss Kelsey. You will be in charge of her daily routine and getting her into bed in the evening. Do you have any questions?"

"Yes. I was hired as a tutor. Even though it appears that my responsibilities have been extended to that of a nanny or even a mother, I view my first priority as being a teacher. Therefore, where will the classes be conducted? Is there a classroom?"

"No ma'am, but if you have a problem, I suggest you take it up with the ambassador."

"Very well, then, I'll need to speak with the ambassador when he finishes with Kelsey," she informed the maid.

"Oh, I'm afraid that won't be possible. He's already late leaving for the office, and he abhors being late. You'll just have to wait until this evening when he comes home." She had turned to leave when Natalie raised her voice.

"I guess you didn't understand me when I said I'll need to see him before he leaves. In fact, I demand to see him for a couple minutes before he leaves and I want you to inform him. Do you hear me?"

"Yes, Miss Holmes, I hear you," a deep voice spoke softly just behind her.

Natalie whirled around, sucking in her breath as she took a step backward.

"Oh, I didn't know you were there," she stammered.

"I can well imagine that you didn't," he agreed, staring down at her with impatience emanating from deep-set eyes under eyebrows drawn together in a frown, marring his otherwise-handsome face.

"I mean that I didn't hear you. I don't mean that I wouldn't have insisted on meeting with you had I known you were there." When his expression remained the same and he didn't speak, she rushed on. "All I want to know is where I can find the original teacher's study plan, and I'll need a room where I can set up a classroom."

"What precious little the former teacher left is in the green folder on the small desk in your room. As to a classroom, I'll have to check in to the possibility of converting the small bedroom next to Kelsey's. It's not large, but then I guess it doesn't have to be. Will that do until I get home this evening?" His facial expression hadn't changed; just his eyebrows had gone from being pulled together in irritation to arching over his eyes, almost daring her to argue with him.

"Yes, that will do fine. I'll just spend the day getting to know Kelsey."

As he stepped around her, she thought of one more question.

"Excuse me just a moment." He hesitated, only looking over his shoulder at her like she was now becoming a nuisance. "I wanted to know what punishment you had given to Kelsey so I can enforce it."

He continued to stare at her for a couple more moments before answering. "I told her to stay in my room for the next hour, and then you would be coming to get her for her lessons." After a pause, he added one last jab. "Now, will you allow me to get on with my business?"

Inside she was fuming, but she managed to just nod her head. When he and the maid had disappeared from the hall she stomped into her room, shutting the door before venting some of her anger by throwing her purse across the room to land on the bed.

She hadn't been this angry since her brother George had shut the cat in the cellar and then told her a rabid dog had carried off the poor little thing. She almost smiled at how silly it sounded now, but when she was six years old, she tended to believe what she was told. She had been devastated. It was only a small concession that Grandpa had taken him out behind the barn to "talk" to him.

She looked around the room for the first time and was awestruck by the beauty. The ceilings were at least ten feet high with 10-inch crown molding finishing off the wallpaper that gave the room a Victorian look. Small flowers in pale green against the cream-colored paper lent the perfect contrast to the white wrought iron canopy bed covered with a white eyelet spread and numerous pillows in green, yellow, and white—some plain and some in the same printed material as the drapes.

Against one wall was a white rocker and a small table with a lamp set to the perfect height to sit and read, while a five-drawer dresser was tucked into a corner alcove.

She turned at the light tap on the bedroom door.

"Yes?"

Andrew opened the door and stepped inside with her luggage.

"Is the room satisfactory, ma'am?"

"Oh, Andrew, it's like a small garden just waiting for me to sit down with a good book and enjoy it," she beamed, taking the cosmetic case.

"Well, you just let me or Clyde know if you need anything, and we'll take care of it for you," he promised, saluting with two fingers to the brim of his cap before stepping back into the hall and pulling the door shut.

She glanced around once again. The anger from a minute ago was gone and forgotten as she headed for the bathroom that she could see through an open door on the far side of the room.

She was washing her hands when she glanced up in the mirror and saw the bedroom door start to open. Turning, she saw the tiny girl, her mass of auburn hair bouncing as she quickly ducked inside the room and shut the door quietly behind her.

The cherub face had huge blue eyes like her father, eyes that were now searching out the room. "Hello?" She took a couple dainty steps forward into the room, calling out in a voice just above a whisper.

Natalie made just enough noise to draw the child's gaze before she spoke.

"Hi. I'm Natalie Holmes," she announced, stepping from the bathroom into the bedroom to greet the young visitor.

Kelsey was startled for just a moment before the most brilliant smile Natalie had ever seen lit up the little girl's face.

"Hello, Miss Natalie. I'm very pleased to make your acquaintance," she stated formally. "Are you my new teacher?" Before Natalie could answer, the child continued. "Because if you are, I don't understand. My daddy's social secretary, Miss Jennifer, told me that you were much older, with gray hair and a bad back. She told me that I wouldn't be able to get you to take me outside to play and I couldn't, in all politeness, ask you to go swimming or hiking with me. But you're not old. In fact, you're pretty. I don't understand," she finished on a deep frown, flopping back against the side of Natalie's bed.

"Well, I'm also glad to make your acquaintance, and you're right, I'm not old and gray-haired, so I'm not sure who or what Miss Jennifer was talking about. But all that aside, I'm happy to finally meet you," she said, sticking out her hand to shake with the little girl.

The child giggled as she stuck her hand in Natalie's.

"Only big people shake hands and I'm not big yet. You're funny," she laughed.

"Some people say you're only as old as you feel. I think you're as old as you act." Natalie stood staring down at the cherub who smiled at her with such innocence. "Am I mistaken or did I hear your father say that you were to stay in his room for an hour and then I'd come get you to work on your lessons?"

The smile disappeared and her head slowly bent, her eyes lowering to the carpet. "I was hoping you didn't know about that." She toed the carpet for a few moments before turning her head slightly to look up at Natalie. "It's not fun in his room, so I wanted to be in here with you," she admitted.

Natalie felt so sorry for the motherless child. She seemed to need love and attention and her punishment was to spend an hour alone. That didn't seem fair, but since she had asked and had been told what the punishment was, she couldn't very well ignore it or cancel it.

"Well, I have a suggestion. Why don't I take the folder concerning your work and maybe a story book, and we'll use the hour in your father's room to get to know each other?"

The little head snapped up, the bright smile back in place.

"Oh, right. That's jolly good. I'll grab a book and meet you in his room." She opened the door and scampered down the hall, happy now that she didn't have to do penitence alone.

"Well, this might not be the smartest decision I've ever made, but what's done is done. If I have to face the firing squad, so be it," she whispered as she grabbed the green folder and left the room.

Chapter Two

The long day was finally over and all he could think about was getting home so he could sit outside in the garden for a short while before dinner, maybe with a glass of Chablis.

The delegate from Russia had droned on for what seemed like hours, until numerous members, himself included, had started yawning.

As the limousine rounded the curve that brought the house into view, Trenton smiled with satisfaction. He never tired of coming home. He missed England, but the rolling hills of Westchester County were perfectly suited for Kelsey and him.

When he had first accepted the position at the United Nations, he had kept an apartment in a high-rise. When his wife died, he knew the city was not a good place to raise a child, especially one with as much energy as Kelsey.

It had only taken the real estate agent two weeks to find the perfect solution. The estate boasted fifteen acres of rolling grassy lawn dotted with groves of trees to break the landscape. It had allowed him to live near enough to the city to commute, yet keep the feel of the countryside like that of his childhood home in England. He couldn't believe his good luck in finding just the right house so quickly when he had needed it.

"Here we are, sir. Will you be needing the car any more this evening?"

"No, thanks, Andrew. I'll see you in the morning." He stepped out of the car, oblivious to everything else around him as he mentally focused on one of the files he had brought home with him to read before the meeting resumed tomorrow.

"Daddy!" The little girl slipped through the door and was halfway down the stairs, her legs pumping to get her to the destination as soon as possible.

"Careful," he called out as he dropped his briefcase on the asphalt so he could grab the child and swing her up in a high arch. Her laughter filled the air as her arms flared out like a plane and she threw her head back.

"Fly me high, Daddy. Higher!" Her father twirled her around in a circle, a loud, deep laugh booming out from deep in his chest to dance with her delighted giggles.

"Flight KL-5 coming in for a landing," he said, his eyes still glued to the little girl now dropping from the sky, safe in the arms of her father who would never let her fall.

"Can we do it again?" She always begged, but he seldom gave her a second 'flight.'

"I'm tired, honey." He picked up this briefcase. "Did you have a good day?"

"Oh yes. I quite like the new tutor. She is a lot of fun and smarter than the last one," she finished, tucking her small hand in her father's as they climbed the stairs together.

"Oh? In what way is she smarter?"

"She seems to know what I'm thinking . . . before I even think of it," she announced emphatically.

"Well, Kell-bell, that's a good thing. That means you won't be able to pull the wool over her eyes." He laughed, stopping to push open the door so she could walk through ahead of him.

"Why would I put wool on her eyes?" Kelsey screwed up her face as she thought about the unusual thing her father had just suggested. "You're funny, Daddy," she decided, pulling her hand loose and darting toward the office.

"Daddy, will you be home tonight?" She entered his office, making a beeline for his desk where she hoisted herself into the seat and used her foot against the desk to start the chair turning in a circle.

"Keep your feet off the furniture," he admonished automatically, laying the case on the desk.

"But I have to if I'm going to twirl. My legs won't reach the floor."

When her comment was met with silence she allowed the chair to wind to a stop, staring up at her father who was now frowning.

"Sorry. I'll try to remember." She ducked her chin, hoping she hadn't made him angry. She didn't want to ruin the special dinner the cook had planned for Miss Natalie's first night.

"It's okay," he smiled, reaching down to pick up the child, his long fingers digging into her ribs on her way up from the chair.

Her feet were kicking and her laughter intermixed with her pleas for him to stop. When he stood her on the floor, he leaned over to put his face near hers.

"Now, what I need you to do is run along and I'll see you at dinner. I have a couple calls to make and some work to look over before then." He tweaked her nose as she scrunched up her shoulders and giggled.

"Okay, Daddy. I'll go see what Miss Natalie is doing and ask if she needs me to take her to the dining room. Bye," she waved over her shoulder as she breezed out the door and down the hall toward the stairs.

". . . and then we came out to the kitchen and Miss Carmen gave us both a snack," the little girl said, stuffing another bite of pudding in her mouth. "And then we . . ."

"Kelsey, don't talk with your mouth full," admonished her father.

Natalie was glad to see that he didn't lose his temper and yell at his daughter, rather reminded her of the rules in a calm, soft-spoken tone.

"Well, little lady, it sounds like you had a full day and your new teacher is doing her job well," he added, his eyes shifting to Natalie.

"Oh yes, Daddy. She even made Miss Carmen like her and everyone knows how grouchy Miss Carmen can be." The moment the words were spoken, the youngster sucked in her breath and looked over at her father through long lashes.

"I think you've said enough and I think it's time you excused yourself and went up to your room to bathe for bed. I'm sure Miss Natalie will be up directly to check on you." The look he was giving his daughter wasn't mean, just direct, and she knew he meant business since she complied without any argument.

"Excuse me, please," she whispered, sliding out of the chair and quietly slipping out the door of the large dining room, her eyes downcast.

Natalie felt sorry for the little girl, but knew she had to learn when to keep her thoughts to herself and when to talk. At least Mr. Lancaster had been receptive about her constant stream of words during the meal, even encouraging her to tell him more.

Natalie hadn't made up her mind yet, but so far she

thought he was a good father. Now if he turned out to be as good an employer, she'd be a happy person.

"So, Miss Holmes, how would you say your first day went?" He didn't look up, but continued to butter another fluffy biscuit, adding a dollop of apricot jam before lifting it to take a bite as his eyes rose to meet hers.

"I'd say it went well. I've had a chance to go over what there was of a lesson plan and I've got several ideas on additional areas of instruction that I feel she needs." She watched him chewing, his jaw flexing as he took another bite. He could easily put her in a trance if she wasn't careful.

"If you'd like," she continued, clearing her throat, "I'll work up a plan tonight and give you a copy in the morning before you leave for work." Her food was totally forgotten as she sat with her hands folded in her lap. She felt like a naughty child sitting before the principal, but forced herself to relax her shoulders and reach for her fork. She wanted nothing more than to make a success of this job. She loved Kelsey and the home and someday this position would look great on her resume.

"That sounds reasonable. Then I'd like a weekly progress report and I'd like you to clear it with me when you want to take her from the estate." He saw her stiffen, but ignored it as he continued.

"I try to keep a low-profile security system around Kelsey, but in today's times I must be cautious. Your

American FBI has told me that, because of some committee work that I do, there has been some recent credible threats to my safety and that of my family. I can't afford to take chances on the safety of my family, which," he added with a slight smile, "now includes you, Miss Holmes."

Natalie was surprised that he would consider her in his security plans, but after thinking about it for a few moments she figured it made sense. After all, if she had Kelsey with her, then they would both need to be protected.

"Okay, but I'd like to have a little freedom to take Kelsey on some field trips, unless you have already taken her to the Statue of Liberty and the Empire State Building?"

"No, I haven't had the time yet. Yes, that would be good for her. Work out a date and let me know. Andrew has been with me for the past ten years and is responsible for all security, so if there's ever a problem, please tell him. And by all means, do whatever he instructs you. He was trained at Scotland Yard," he finished up.

Natalie was speechless for a moment while she let his words sink in. She would never have figured a squat man of approximately five inches over five feet being a member of Scotland Yard. She had always mentally pictured them as the tall, dashing, 007-type guys. She had to broaden her thinking.

"Since you live way out here, I guess I hadn't given

thought to there being any danger, but I appreciate you telling me."

"Maybe even more caution has to be taken since we live way out here. If anything ever happens, it will take the police longer to respond than in Midtown Manhattan."

His eyes followed her every move, mesmerized by the woman who had invaded his home and his thoughts since he first met her that morning. When his secretary had told him that a new tutor had been hired from the approved list, she had implied that the woman was older. Needless to say, he had been stunned when he had been introduced to Natalie. She looked like she had just finished college. She had an innocent, nonworldly appeal that was refreshing after some of the thick-skinned professional women he had to deal with on a daily basis.

"Well, sir, if you'll excuse me I think I'll go upstairs and help Kelsey with her bath and get her into bed." When he nodded, she stood and left him alone in the dining room.

He sat staring at the huge mirror that hung on the far wall behind the table. As he looked at his reflection, sitting at the table alone, he couldn't help but remember happier times; times when Sarah had been alive and they had laughed and loved. But those times had died over the years, leaving him alone even before his wife was killed in the car accident.

Only he knew the real truth. He had found her journal. There was only one reason that Kelsey had not been with her mother that day, only one reason that the child was still alive. If Sarah had not been meeting her true love, the child would no doubt have been snatched from him along with his wife.

It didn't matter that she had been his wife in name only ever since Kelsey had been born; it was still a shock when she was so violently killed. It also didn't matter that she hadn't been alone in the car, but someday Kelsey would probably learn the truth. He figured he would deal with that when the time came.

Trenton glanced down at his wine as he rolled the liquid around in the bottom of the glass. He should have known. He should have recognized the signs that she was unhappy with their marriage and ripe for another man to pluck, but he had been too busy. He had not even been around when she was crying herself to sleep years ago, nor there when she started getting attention elsewhere. Sometimes he wished she hadn't left a journal. It might have been easier to wonder about the man in the car with her.

He shoved his hands through his hair before heaving a sigh and standing.

"Can I get you anything else, sir?" The maid appeared carrying a carafe of coffee.

"No, thanks," he dismissed the woman before turning to head to his office. He had to put those days behind him and face the fact that he was alone in the world with Kelsey. His two priorities were Kelsey and his job with the United Nations. In that order.

But somehow he couldn't get the picture of bright blue eyes and dark blond hair out of his mind. The woman had just arrived and already she was a distraction.

"So the big bad wolf huffed and puffed, but he couldn't blow down the little pig's brick house," Natalie said.

"Is that the end of the story?"

"Well," Natalie said, smiling. "I guess we could say that they lived happily ever after, safe in their brick home," she finished up.

"Wow. That was good. I'm sure glad we don't live in a house made of straw or wood. I wouldn't want him to blow my house down," she frowned at the thought.

"Him who?" Came a masculine voice.

"Daddy!"

"I was wondering who might be planning to blow our house down," he frowned, as he walked over to the bed where Kelsey now squatted on her knees, her hands outstretched toward her father.

"The big bad wolf, silly," she giggled, snuggling her face into his neck. "You smell pretty," she said against his skin.

"Well, thank you very much, little one," he hugged her tight before sitting her back in bed. "And we must thank Miss Holmes for telling you such loving stories right before you go to sleep. I'm sure it will help you to sleep without any disturbances," he said to the little girl while his words admonished Natalie for her choice of stories.

"Oh, you know it's my favorite story," she laughed, putting her small hands on each side of his face and leaning in for a quick kiss.

"Yes, I do. Now go to sleep. I'll see you tomorrow morning at breakfast." He leaned over to rub his face in her stomach, setting her off again, giggling and screaming for him to stop.

Natalie sat on the edge of the bed looking across at the top of Trenton's head. His wavy hair was as dark as Kelsey's, only without the auburn highlights she had seen earlier in the day when they had been outside in the sunlight. She had expected to be working for a stiff-necked English politician who would want little to do with his daughter, putting up with her for a minimum amount of time each day and not really caring how she was doing in school as long as she didn't embarrass the family name by flunking out of grade level. As she watched the interaction between father and daughter, she realized how wrong she had been.

"Miss Natalieeee," she squealed. "Help me!" Her laughter and screams were reverberating off the wall as she begged, bucking and kicking her legs, her tiny hands digging into his thick hair and trying to pull his head away.

Natalie hesitated for a moment before throwing caution to the wind. Without giving thought to the long-range ramifications, she grabbed one of his arms and started pulling.

"I'll save you, Kelsey," she laughed as she tugged.

Before she could take her next breath she had been flipped onto her back, and Trenton was stretched across the small bed, his head hovering over hers.

"Look what interfering got you?" His smile was almost sinister as he slowly leaned closer.

She stared up into his face, her eyes growing larger as her heart beat faster. She was helpless, an insect caught in his web, holding her breathe as his focus shifted from her eyes to her lips and then back.

"Daddy! You're supposed to be playing with me, not Miss Natalie. She's too big to play tickle," the child admonished.

He hesitated for another moment before moving away, clearing his throat as he smiled at his daughter. Natalie let out a breath, her chest now heaving as she realized what a stupid thing she had done. She couldn't believe she had grabbed her employer's arm. This was going to have to stop. She wished she could turn back the clock, she thought as she sat up, pushing her hair back from her face before standing to put space between them.

"Kelsey," she choked out, "I'll see you in the morning." She was almost to the door and unable to stop herself from glancing over her shoulder. Trenton wasn't even looking at her.

"Good night." She almost ran from the room. She had made a fool of herself and she had no one else to blame.

What is wrong with me? She knew better than to do anything personal with an employer. She silently berated herself all the way to her room. She couldn't believe she had pulled on his arm. This was probably the shortest employment she had ever had. *He'll fire me tomorrow. That's for sure. How could I have been so stupid?*

It was a long night. She tossed and turned, unable to find a comfortable position until the wee hours, just before someone crawled into bed with her.

Chapter Three

Jerked from sleep, Natalie's body tensed. When a tiny body snuggled up to her, she smiled in the dark and relaxed.

"Are you all right, sweetie?" She whispered so she wouldn't frighten the child as she turned on her side and draped an arm around tiny shoulders.

"I had to go to the bathroom and then I didn't want to get back in bed alone," came the soft muffled voice from near her shoulder.

"Would you like to stay with me until morning?"

A nodded head was the only answer she got. Natalie lay in the dark, her head tucked over until her cheek was resting on the child's soft curls. The fragrance of Kelsey's strawberry shampoo filled her nostrils, taking her mind back to earlier in the evening when she had helped the child bathe and wash her hair.

"Watch me, Miss Natalie," the child ordered, the water in the oval tub rocking gently near her armpits as she sat with her diving goggles on. Without waiting for confirmation, Kelsey flipped onto her stomach and stuck her head below the surface of the water, holding her breath as she looked at the bottom of the tub, turning her head one way and then the other.

She suddenly emerged, sending water flying in all directions as she rose up like a dolphin making a leap. She pulled off the goggles, leaving a red ring indenting her face where the mask had pushed into her skin.

The child laughed out loud as the water rocked violently, sloshing over the rim of the tub to splash onto the tile floor. "Whoops," she giggled, scrunching up her shoulders like she was going to duck under the water again.

"I think we've made just about enough mess for one night, don't you agree?"

"No, I love the water. Miss Mattie doesn't mind cleaning up the bathroom. She told me she loves it," she said, pulling the mask back over her matted hair.

"I rather doubt she loves cleaning the bathroom. I'd sooner think she loves you and therefore is willing to clean up the mess you make. Is that closer to what she said?"

"Something like that. She was smiling, so I know she

wasn't angry with me. That's all that counts, right?" Again she dove under the water, the waves rocking up near the edge.

Natalie had to smile at the child's deduction, but if allowed to continue, Kelsey would be a very spoiled and bratty teenager. She would have to work on getting the child to think about others a little more and how much they did for her. She needed to get her in the habit of thanking others for what they did. Starting tonight.

When bath time was over, she wrapped the little girl in a huge towel, her hair in a smaller one, and sat her down on the edge of the tub that was now gurgling as it emptied.

"Kelsey, I need you to do something for me." She watched to be sure the child was listening before she continued. "Have you noticed that your father thanks people when they do things for him? Like when Andrew holds open the car door, your father thanks him. Have you noticed?"

"Um hum. He says thank you all the time." She sat kicking her feet back and forth, hindered only by the folds of terry cloth wrapped around her legs.

"Well, I think it's something you should start doing too. All young ladies do it and it will show your father that you are growing up."

"Okay. Do you see how my toes are pruney?" She stuck out her feet to show Natalie her wrinkled skin. Lesson over, apparently.

"Come on, let's get you dressed." Leading the way

across the hall to her bedroom, Natalie saw the maid coming down the hallway. "I'm sorry for the mess in the bathroom," Natalie called out. She saw the woman frown slightly.

"But thank you for cleaning it up," piped up a small voice behind her.

Natalie had the pleasure of seeing the maid's mouth drop open just before entering Kelsey's bedroom. "Kill 'em with kindness," she whispered to herself, quoting an adage her mother lived by.

Now she had the little cherub snuggled up to her, trusting her tutor to protect her from all the scary monsters that came out at night. But who was going to protect the tutor from the temptation to think of herself as mother to this little girl? The child was so sweet and so open and friendly. She was easy to love. But if she were Kelsey's mother, then that would make Trenton her husband. Whee, that was some thought. He was the type of man that dreams were made of. Pure "tall, dark and handsome" kind of stuff right out of the movies.

She had a hard time thinking of him as simply Trenton Lancaster when he held a position that separated the two of them by a country mile. She had grown up in the backwoods of West Virginia and he had grown up in a mansion in England. Or at least she figured he had lived in a mansion. He seemed used to servants and having everything done for him, where she was just trying to wrap her mind around having a driver who would take her and Kelsey wherever they wanted to go.

Well, it would work out, assuming that Mr. Lancaster didn't fire her for being so impertinent as to join in on their tussling match. She drifted to sleep with thoughts of a dark-haired prince riding up on a black steed to whisk her away to his castle.

Downstairs was a buzz of activity, a vacuum already being run in a back room of the house when Trenton came downstairs for breakfast. By now Kelsey usually accosted him for a ride down the stairs, but her bedroom door was still closed. Strange.

He ate his normal breakfast of oatmeal, fruit, and toast, but still Kelsey had not made an appearance. Was she sick?

He stood, folded the morning paper, and set it on the edge of the table before heading up the stairs and into the child's room. He felt a slight chill slide down his back when he saw the bed empty with its rumpled sheets. A quick glance across the hall told him that she wasn't in the bathroom. He immediately turned toward the tutor's room, Natalie's room. No, it was safer to think of her as the tutor. Could Kelsey be in there?

The door was open about an inch, enabling him to peek inside. After a moment's hesitation, he pushed open the door and silently walked over to the bed where he stood staring down at the two laying asleep.

The contrast between the beautiful honey-haired

woman and the auburn curls of his daughter was striking. He had trouble dragging his eyes away from the
lightly freckled skin that showed where her nightgown
scooped low, exposing a few inches of skin. He had no
business being here and couldn't even imagine how embarrassed he'd feel if she opened her eyes and saw him
staring down at her. The blanket was down to her waist,
displaying her slender form for his eyes to feast on.

He jerked himself around and headed for the door.
What in the world was he thinking about? He always
thought of himself as a gentleman, but he had just thrown
that distinction out the window. His mind was churning,
his breath coming in choppy pants as he quietly closed
the door behind him, shutting the image of his daughter
in the arms of the beautiful tutor from his view. It took
only a moment to realize that the picture was imbedded
in his brain. He knew it would haunt him.

"Damn," he muttered as he ran his hand over his face
and headed for the stairs. He'd just have to keep busy
today. Very busy.

Natalie's heart was pounding like it wanted out of
her chest. She could hardly believe that she had been
able to lie still enough to convince Mr. Lancaster that she
was asleep. It was a wonder he hadn't heard her heart
thumping twice as fast as normal or seen it pounding
against her ribcage. When he had stopped by the door,
she had barely had her eyes open, trying to get used to

the light and savoring the moment before she had to move and risk waking the child.

Kelsey was so warm and sweet, but the child was lying across her arm and her arm and hand were numb. Not to mention that she desperately needed to use the bathroom. That was when she had seen Trenton step up to the door. She had closed her eyes, waiting for him to move on past so she could get up and close the door.

She hadn't heard him move to the bedside, but she could feel his presence; in fact, she could smell his musky aftershave. She knew he was standing over the bed, looking down at Kelsey and her. She concentrated on not moving a muscle, the arm under the child drawing most of her attention as it began to throb in earnest.

He didn't stay long, but each second was agonizing. Not just her arm that was aching, but knowing that she didn't have much on, not even make-up. She felt vulnerable, exposed. She was tempted to open her eyes, but after last night and now this morning, she couldn't imagine facing him. She toughed it out until she heard the latch on the door click.

She breathed a silent breath of relief when she opened her eyes a slit and saw that he had left. Thank goodness. How was she ever going to face him again? How embarrassing!

Easing her arm slowly out from under Kelsey's head, she crawled out of bed and made her way on tiptoes to the bathroom connected to her room. She stared at the reflection in the mirror. She looked the same as yesterday, but she certainly didn't feel the same.

After taking care of her immediate needs, she washed her face, brushed her teeth, and her shoulder-length hair, sweeping it up into a ponytail. Today was going to be sultry and warm, and she wanted to be comfortable when she took Kelsey outside for a nature lesson.

"Good morning, Miss Natalie." The cheery voice behind her made her whirl around and smile at the bright-eyed child looking up at her. "Me and you had a sleep over," she beamed. "Only big girls do that. It was fun," she said, lifting her nightgown and hoisting herself up on the toilet. "Can we do it again sometime?"

"Well certainly. But next time maybe we can plan ahead and have hot chocolate in bed and read books until midnight," she smiled.

"Okay!" Finishing, she flushed the toilet before skipping out into the bedroom, ready to take on the new day with renewed energy. She twirled around in a circle, her arms out, and her eyes closed. When she stopped and opened her eyes, she giggled as she wobbled around.

"You're walking pretty unsteady there, mate," Natalie said, laughing along with her. "You're like a drunken sailor." As soon as the words were out of her mouth, she knew Kelsey would want more explanation.

"What do you mean?"

She had stopped twirling, figuring this conversation sounded much more interesting than getting dizzy.

"Well," Natalie hesitated, "have you heard about pirates and pirate ships?"

"Um hum. I saw the movie about Captain Hook and Peter Pan."

Great! "Okay, it's like when they walk on the deck of a ship that's at sea and they kind of wobble around while they walk because the ship is going up and down with the waves," she finished. Well, that wasn't entirely true, but it was good enough for a five-year-old.

"Oh, I understand. I thought you were talking about them drinking too much rum," she said, twirling around again. "Yo-ho-ho and a bottle of rum," she sang out as she stopped and wobbled.

Oh brother, she thought. "Let's get dressed so we can go down for some breakfast," she suggested, hoping to distract her from the pirate song.

"Oh, I wanted to tell Daddy that I didn't dream about the wolf blowing down the house," she scampered to the door.

"I think he's already gone."

"How do you know?"

"Well, it's after eight and he usually leaves by eight o'clock, right?" She opened a drawer to pull out a tank top and a pair of denim shorts.

"Oh, you're right," she slumped her shoulders, looking at the floor. Suddenly her head snapped up. "Maybe we can drive in and meet him for lunch," she suggested. "I love to eat in the embassy dining room. They make me drinks with the name of that little girl with curly hair like mine. I can't remember her name," she frowned, chewing her fingernail.

"You mean a Shirley Temple?" She reached over and gently pulled Kelsey's finger down, smiling into the up-turned eyes.

"Yes, that's her! They're good and I get a little um-brella and two cherries," she beamed.

"I suggest that we spend the day here, but we can call your daddy's secretary and set up a date with him to-morrow for lunch." She saw the disappointment on the child's face and rushed to draw her attention away from sad thoughts.

"In fact, I had planned a nature walk in the woods and a picnic lunch out on the hillside for today. What do you think?"

"Can I catch a butterfly?" The smile was back, her hands clapping together excitedly.

"I can't promise, but we can try," she smiled. "Now off to your room and put on some shorts and sandals. And grab a sweater since it might be chilly in the woods," she called out to the child who was already running down the hall toward her room, her auburn curls flying behind her like a flag.

A smile creased her face as memories flooded her mind. Like Kelsey, she had lost a parent while she was young, but just like this precious little girl, Natalie's life had been happy and filled with love.

She quickly dressed, barely getting her tennis shoes

on and tied before Kelsey could be heard running down the hall.

"I'm ready, but I need you to tie my shoes, please."

If she had doubted for one moment that she would be good at this job or that she would be happy as a live-in tutor, all her doubts fled as she knelt down and tied the laces.

"You know, I think this is one of the first things I'll teach you. You need to be able to tie your own shoes. Okay?"

"Okay," she said, tucking her tiny hand in Natalie's as they headed down the stairs toward today's adventure.

Within half an hour they had eaten and the cook had prepared a picnic basket for them to lug along when they went down to the grove of trees.

As they headed out the front door, Clyde came around the side of the house.

"Excuse me, ma'am, but you can't go out on the grounds without an escort," he told her as he reached for the basket.

"Oh?" Her first inner response was irritation. Didn't they trust her? Her frown gradually evaporated as she re-membered that Trenton and his family could possibly be the target of radicals. Growing up with three older broth-ers meant there had been many times that she had fought for independence. This was not a time to be stubborn.

"Yes, ma'am. It's better to be safe than sorry, I always say," he smiled. He was a little older than Andrew, his shoulders stooping slightly as his arm stretched out, indicating they should precede him toward the woods. "Just pretend I'm not here and enjoy your day."

The morning passed quickly with Kelsey's mind soaking up facts about plants and animals like a sponge. They had hiked a couple miles by noon and all were ready to stop for lunch.

It took only a few minutes to spread the blanket and soon the three of them were having sandwiches under the shade of a tree on the crest of one of the hills. They had both insisted that Clyde join them for lunch, finally convincing him that he would hurt their feelings if he didn't accept.

"So how long have you worked for Mr. Lancaster?"

His weathered face crinkled into a quick smile. Fingers gnarled with arthritis lifted the cowboy hat from his head to allow the slight breeze to flutter the few wisps of hair sprinkled on his freckled head. He repositioned the hat before answering.

"I've been here since before he bought the house. I worked for the Michaels who owned it before and when Mr. Lancaster bought it, I was here still taking care of the stables until the horses could be moved, and he asked me if I'd like to stay and put together a good stable for him as well. I love horses and was grateful to be able to stay since I've been living in the little house over the stables for the past ten years." He reached for more grapes before continuing.

"I taught the former owner's children to ride and I'd be happy to teach Miss Kelsey here just as soon as you think she's ready."

"Learn to ride? Me?" Kelsey had been quiet for the past few minutes, happy to arrange her grapes in different designs on her paper plate. Now she was alert, all her attention focused on her tutor. She now faced Natalie, her heart in her eyes as she begged.

"Please can I learn?" She was up on her knees, her hands clasped together as if in prayer as she bargained. "I'll be good and clean up my toys before I go to bed and I'll remember to thank everyone who does something for me, just like you told me to," she added on for good measure. "Please?" She had scooted closer, reaching out to clamp sticky grape juice fingers on Natalie's arm as she pleaded silently with her eyes. "Please," she mouthed again, no sound coming out.

How could she turn down the child's plea? She could remember a similar scene when she had been younger and had wanted a kitten. She had promised everything she could think of to convince her mother, but the answer had still been no. She could still feel the disappointment and the overwhelming loss of something she had never even gotten.

"I think it's a good idea, but . . ." she stressed, holding up one finger when the child jumped up and started dancing around. "I have to ask your father first, so don't get your hopes up too high until I have his answer," she instructed.

"Oh, he won't care," she beamed. "He gives me anything I want. I just have to be polite and say please and thank you." Her eyes were beaming with anticipation, convinced that her heart's desire would soon be a reality.

Natalie had seen the devotion of the father and might not have worried about his answer except that Clyde wasn't smiling. "Is there a problem, Clyde?"

"Not exactly, ma'am. I just think you should know that Mr. Lancaster's brother was killed when he was thrown from a horse when the boys were small. Mr. Lancaster still rides, in fact he brings folks out to ride with him on occasion, but I wanted to warn you. In fact, I probably shouldn't have told you in front of the little princess. Now her hopes are up and if he should have a problem with it, then it will be my fault that she's disappointed. I'm really sorry," he said, touching the back of Natalie's hand.

"I'm sure it'll be fine." Brave words, when her insides were quaking. Her brothers always said that she tended to jump into the deep end, usually before looking to see if there was water in the pool. Had she jumped in already? "I'll speak with him tonight and let you know. Is there a smaller horse available besides the Morgan?"

"No, but I have a nephew who raises ponies and I'm sure I could get a good one at a reasonable price for her to start learning on."

"Okay, why don't you check on that for me," she smiled reassuringly. "I'll speak with Mr. Lancaster this evening. I'll ask him to let you know about the pony."

Kelsey was still dancing around, her arms up in the

air. "I already know what I want to name him," Kelsey said, dancing back to the blanket with a wild flower in her hand. "I'll name my pony Chester."

"Chester?"

"Um hum, my last nanny read me a book once called *Chester, The Friendly Horse,* so I want to name him Chester," she said emphatically.

"But, what if it's a girl horse?"

She stopped for a moment and thought before she smiled. "Chelsey. I like the name Chelsey and it even rhymes with my name. Kelsey and Chelsey. Perfect!"

Soon she was exhausted and sank onto the blanket, flopping back to stare up through the limbs. "Me and Chester will ride like the wind," she laughed out loud, turning on her stomach and propping her chin on her palms. "Someday I'll be able to ride my dad's horse, Thunder, and we'll go faster than the wind!" She rolled onto her back again to watch the clouds.

Natalie could see how excited the child was. She only hoped that Mr. Lancaster would be open to his daughter learning to ride, especially at such an early age. She sent a quick prayer heavenward.

"Okay, gang, let's pack up the left-over food, fold the blanket, and head back toward the house. We have some school work to do," she said, stroking the dark curls as the child moaned her dismay at having to leave.

"So, how was your day?"

"Oh we went on a nature walk and I learned all about

the trees and the birds, and then we sat on the hillside under a tree and had lunch. We had a picnic along with Mr. Clyde who was watching out for us," Kelsey answered without looking up. She was too busy trying to roll a noodle over so she could take another huge bite of lasagna.

Oh no. She had forgotten to tell Kelsey not to mention the riding lessons and to let her talk with Mr. Lancaster first. Fear slammed into her brain and raced down her spine. She turned stricken eyes toward her employer, even before Kelsey continued.

Trenton glanced at Natalie, frowning slightly in confusion as he took an extra moment to stare before refocusing on his daughter when she continued, pausing for only a moment mid-sentence to swallow.

"Then Mr. Clyde offered to teach me to ride and Miss Natalie said she thought it was a good idea and now Mr. Clyde is going to look for a pony for me," she finished, all smiles as she turned toward her father, wiping the back of her hand across her mouth and smearing marinara sauce across her cheek. Her smile faltered when she saw him glaring at Miss Natalie. Pushing her peas around on her plate, she kept busy hiding some under the edge of a noodle before looking up again at her father

"Is something wrong?" Her question came out in a tiny voice as she lowered her arms and put her hands in her lap. When no one spoke she looked down at her hands, closing her eyes as disappointment swamped

her. She wasn't going to get a pony. She knew the look
that her father was giving Miss Natalie. She had seen it
before when the last nanny asked him about getting a
puppy, and a pony was a lot bigger than a puppy.

"May I be excused?" The request was softly spoken,
but she didn't wait for permission to leave the table. She
slipped from the room, not wanting to make her father
more angry by crying and stomping her feet. She would
do that in her room by herself, she vowed, running up
the stairs and down the hall to slam her bedroom door.

Trenton glanced toward the stairs just as the door
slammed. "Happy? Now you've disappointed her. She's
upset and it's entirely your fault," he scolded.

"I beg your pardon, but I'm not the one who disappointed her. You have horses and you ride them, so why
wouldn't you want her to learn to ride? And if you have
a problem with it, why didn't you tell me in advance so
I could have handled it differently?" Natalie instantly
decided not to allow him to blame her if he had a problem with horses. If the child was not going to be allowed
to ride, then why did he have horses on the property? It
didn't make sense and it certainly wasn't fair. Do what I
say, not what I do.

"So now it's my fault because you went behind my
back and got her all excited about having a horse when
you hadn't asked me in advance?"

"No, that's not how it happened at all. Mr. Clyde mentioned that he had kept the stables for the former owners
and continued on with you, setting up your stable and

caring for your horses. Then he said that he'd love to teach Kelsey and when she enthusiastically begged to learn, I said I thought it was a good idea. Which I still think is a good idea," she added, narrowing her eyes to glare at the unreasonable man. "I told her that I'd have to talk with you first and not to get her hopes up."

He was silent for a long time. Natalie's heart rate had spiked when Kelsey first opened her mouth about the horse, but it was beginning to settle down. She took a deep breath, vowing silently to keep control of her tongue. She wouldn't say another word until he did. She didn't have to defend herself any further since she had done nothing wrong.

As the time stretched into minutes where they sat just staring at each other, she began to wonder how this impasse was going to end.

"Do you ride, Miss Natalie?"

"No,' she answered emphatically, a small nervous laugh slipping out as she answered him. She instantly knew she had answered too quickly. She felt a weakness spread through her body as she anticipated what he would say next.

"Well, then it's settled," he leaned back in his chair and laid his napkin on the table. "Kelsey will start lessons when you do."

Chapter Four

The first few days of riding lessons had left Natalie very sore and very angry at Trenton. If he hadn't pushed her back against a wall, she would never have gotten on a horse, let alone more than once. Why did anyone want to ride them? They were big and powerful and smelled. They also attracted flies, and the only thing she hated more than snakes were flies. Even the thought of a snake made her shudder. She and Indiana Jones had one thing in common, that was for sure. As for flies, they carried all kinds of germs that she didn't want around her. But right now Trenton Lancaster was making a rapid assent to the top of her list of things she disliked.

When she came down to dinner each evening she tried to walk without limping, and she would have loved to bring a pillow to sit on, but there was no way she was going to admit to him how much pain she was in.

When she got to the dining room she stopped, took a deep breath, and stood tall as she walked to the table. Her mother had raised her to be strong and not show her brothers her Achilles' heel. The training was standing her in good stead.

She glanced up once to see Trenton watching her, but she refused to acknowledge him or engage him in conversation. For the past three days she had spoken to him only when absolutely necessary, and he had seemed content to eat his dinner in silence except for Kelsey's continual chatter.

Even though she wasn't speaking to him, it didn't mean that she didn't sneak peeks at him when she figured he'd be watching Kelsey. She couldn't seem to stop staring at his profile. His jaw was strong, his Adam's apple bobbing up and down when he laughed at something Kelsey said that struck him funny. His hair was streaked with just a hint of gray running through the brown at his temples, giving him the distinguished look that was expected when she remembered that he was an ambassador. Sometimes it slipped her mind that he worked at the United Nations, especially when he was sitting at the dining table in denim jeans and a sport shirt.

She had been surprised the first time he had come to dinner dressed casually. She had expected Trenton to dress a little more formally for dinner every night, at least leave on his suit until after the meal. In fact, she had packed expecting to have to wear dresses. After all, wasn't that what English aristocrats did in books? She had expected to be extremely underdressed, but she was happy to see that her slacks and blouses worked just fine.

The child was so excited about her new pony that she didn't seem to notice that Natalie was talking only to her and not to her father. Chester was the most beautiful, the fastest, and the smartest pony to ever live and she had her father to thank for getting it for her.

On the third night, Natalie was almost finished eating when Trenton struck.

"I say, Natalie, how are the riding lessons going?" He had finished and had leaned back in his chair, like he was just passing the time of day.

"They're going fine," she answered without bothering to look up from her plate.

"Actually, Daddy, she's pretty sore," Kelsey chimed in. Before Natalie could stop her, she continued. "In fact she was crying the second day when she got back from the trot across the field," she stated matter-of-factly.

Natalie wished it were possible to slink under the table and disappear. Why in the world had Kelsey said that? She hadn't even thought the child noticed. She could feel her face flushing with heat, but she refused to say another word. She straightened her shoulders and faced him.

His eyes jerked from his daughter to pin Natalie like a bug in the clutches of a spider. As he narrowed his eyes, he allowed the slightest of grins to creep across his lips.

"Well, well, well. So you've been lying to me, is that right?" He sat with his fingers steepled together, eyeing her like a morsel he was considering devouring. She wouldn't have been surprised if he had licked his lips and rubbed his hands together.

"No, I have never lied to you. You asked how the lessons are going, and Clyde said they're going fine," she answered dogmatically.

His smile was gone and his voice had gotten gruff as he stated the obvious. "But you're sore." When she didn't respond to what he wanted to know, he tried again. "What have you been doing for the sore muscles?" He was now leaning toward her, a slight frown marring his good looks.

He sounded so concerned that she had to take several fortifying breaths before she spoke. "Nothing. Well, I've been taking Tylenol, but nothing else. I don't do drugs if that's what you're insinuating," she hissed through her clamped teeth.

"No, for heaven sake, take off the boxing gloves and settle down. I'm concerned. I thought you'd know enough to at least be using Ben-Gay or something for the sore muscles." His next comment faltered when he saw her face turn pink. "Um, I'll have one of the maids bring you some tonight. It might help," he said, clearing his throat.

Natalie glanced over at Kelsey to see if she was paying attention. The child was riveted to the conversation, intently looking from one adult to the other. For the first time since they had sat down to eat, she was totally silent.

"Natalie, for what it's worth, I'm sorry you're so sore. I didn't think you'd stay on long enough each day to even get sore and since you didn't act like it was hurting you, I didn't . . . well, anyway, I'm sorry," he finished lamely. He could feel his neck and face grow warm, but he refused to look away.

He watched as she lowered her eyes, watching her plate while she moved the last of her food around.

"Kelsey, I think it's time you were excused to go up and get ready for bed. Since you've already had your bath, just get dressed and we'll be up in a couple minutes to read to you and tuck you in, okay?"

Kelsey glanced over at Natalie before answering her father. "All right." She slowly stood and walked out of the room, hesitating at the door to look back once more before heading up the stairs.

He waited until he heard the door at the top of the stairs close before he continued.

"Natalie, look at me." She laid her fork down and put her hands in her lap, but didn't raise her eyes. "Please?" When her eyes rose to meet his, they were purposely blank. He didn't know what she was thinking, but he had to admire her ability to control her emotions. Most women would have cried or thrown a tantrum. She was a remarkable woman.

"Listen, I didn't intend for you to be in pain. I figured you'd do the least possible in order to assure that Kelsey could have lessons." He ran his large fingers through his hair in frustration. "I asked Clyde how you were doing and he said you were doing great. He bragged about how quickly you were learning. I guess I figured he was just saying that so he could continue to teach Kelsey."

When she continued to remain silent, he started to get angry.

"All right. So be angry with me if you want. I know I didn't intend for this to happen and, in fact, it's your own fault. If you hadn't promised Kelsey, then you wouldn't have had to get on the blasted horse and now you wouldn't have sore . . . well, let's just say that you wouldn't be hurting," he finished in a huff. He threw his napkin on the table and stood up to leave.

"I don't blame you," she said softly.

He stopped and turned to look at her. She may have been in pain, but her shoulders were back and she was holding her head high. She wasn't going to allow him to beat her down.

"You may have thrown down the challenge, but I was the one who picked it up and ran with it. I wanted to prove that I could overcome fear and learn to do something that you apparently didn't think I could learn."

She moved up another notch in his admiration. He felt helpless to get her to believe him, but he had to try.

"It wasn't that I figured you *couldn't* learn to ride, I just thought that you *wouldn't*." He wanted to take her in his arms and hold her—try to make her feel better—but she had always kept her distance from him. He supposed it wasn't a good idea to get too emotionally involved with an employee anyway, if he had to be honest with himself, but he felt sorry for her. He'd feel the same if a child or an animal was hurt. He'd want to try to make things better. But when he thought of comforting her, it was nothing like when he soothed his daughter's hurts.

No, this woman was interfering with his concentration. He found her on his mind too often. Why did he imagine running his hands through her hair? Or slipping her into his arms to snuggle her close and kiss those lips that pucker like she's pouting just before she laughed.

The whole horse thing seemed to be backfiring. He had just intended to push her buttons and make her angry. She was beautiful when she was angry. Instead he had pushed her into doing something she didn't want to do and now she was paying for it. Besides, all she had wanted was for his daughter to have the chance to learn to ride and he had blackmailed her, yet she hadn't backed down or cheated. She had lived up to her end of the bargain, even though it had been painful for her. It didn't seem fair, but it was too late now.

"It also might help if you soak in the bathtub in hot water," he suggested. "I'll go up and read to Kelsey. I'll see you in the morning. Oh, and you don't have to take any more lessons," he conceded. "Kelsey can still learn." He stood, leaving her alone at the table as he hesitated at the door before shaking his head and continuing up the stairs.

She was thankful that he left without saying another word. She was so embarrassed for him to know that her rear end was sore that she didn't even want to look him in the eye. Having grown up with three older brothers she never would have thought she would be embarrassed for Trenton to discuss her body, but she was. Somehow, it was different.

She laid her napkin on the table and slowly rose.

"Is there anything else I can get for you?" The little maid stood at the door between the dining room and the kitchen, holding a carafe of coffee.

"Yes," she smiled sheepishly. "I need that carafe of coffee and a cup upstairs in my bathroom and a tube of Ben-Gay."

"Right away, ma'am," she smiled in return.

Ever since the first day, the maid had gradually warmed toward Natalie. The past couple days when she was limping around, Miss Mattie had been actually friendly. Like all the staff, the little maid had a soft spot for the child and everyone was noticing the devotion the new tutor had toward the little girl.

Natalie limped up the stairs and kissed Kelsey good-night before running water in the oval tub and slipping in, lying back until the water covered her entire body. At the light tap on the door, she turned her head.

"Come in."

The maid pushed the door open with her hip, balancing the tray as she came in and sat it on a stool near the tub. She poured a cup of coffee, adding a dollop of cream before stepping out of the room and closing the door.

Now this was the life. She settled back, soon drifting off to sleep.

A knock on the door had her jerking up to sit while barely warm water sloshed around her, lapping over the top of the tub to run down and puddle on the tile floor.

"Natalie?"

"Yes?" She automatically covered herself with her arms at the sound of Trenton's voice. What if he walked into the bathroom?

"Are you okay?" he spoke through the door. "I knocked on your bedroom door and when I didn't get an answer, I got worried."

"I'm fine. I'll be right out,'

"No need. Just as long as I know you're okay. I'll see you in the morning." He stood in her room, the fragrance of her perfume lingering lightly to tease his senses, just enough to invade and fog his thinking.

Why had he knocked on her door? Why was he torturing himself? He knew he had been drawn to her room, but he wasn't sure why he had come inside. Well, he admitted to himself, he *had* made up an excuse in case she had answered her door. He would have shown concern about her sore muscles and asked if she had enough Tylenol.

He had read the mandatory story, gotten Kelsey the required drink of water, and kissed her a dozen times, but all his subconscious had been focused on was what excuse he could use to knock on Natalie's door and talk with her. When he saw the light shining under her door, he stood in the hall several minutes before getting up the nerve to knock.

Now he was headed to his bedroom, with her knowing he had been thinking about her and checking on her. She was making him crazy. Did she know that? Did she care?

In his bathroom he stood staring at himself in the mirror. He looked the same but since she came, he had changed.

"Trenton old buddy, I bet she's in her room right now laughing at you." He hit the wall with the palm of his hand before turning his back on the mirror. She was putting up a barrier between them, a barrier he had to decide if he wanted to breach or not.

She waited for a moment until she faintly heard the door close, letting her know he had left her room. Her shoulders slumped in relief. She hadn't realized that her heart rate had spiked, beating a rhythm on her ribs, but she concentrated on breathing deep and slow until it was back closer to normal.

What was she going to do about him? What *could* she do about him? She was attracted to him; she was starting to have feelings for him and she wasn't sure how to deal with those feelings. Back home if she decided she liked one of the guys, she might have just told him how she felt. That was the accepted way in her small hometown when she was growing up, but this was different. Very different.

She turned the knob to release the water before standing and wrapping a white bath towel around herself. The cool breeze from the air conditioner made chill bumps rise on her skin as she stepped out of the tub and headed to her room to gather her underwear and nightgown, her thoughts never far from Trenton and what she wished could be.

Trenton was thankful that Natalie was all right, but the entire situation had left him feeling unraveled. The woman was driving him crazy. He stuffed his hands in his pockets and wandered aimlessly down the hall toward the door leading out to the balcony. He had stood in the middle of his bedroom for quite a while, just thinking about the tutor and the changes she had made in his and Kelsey's life in such a short time. He knew he would be unable to sleep if he went to bed.

He couldn't stop his mind from replaying the scene in Natalie's bedroom when he had been looking for Kelsey that morning. He was ashamed of himself for invading her privacy by standing over her to stare at her sleeping in the bed. He had no excuse for his behavior.

Frustrated with not being able to relax his mind, he continued on his way to the balcony where he could enjoy the cool breeze that had blown away the day's heat. On his way down the hall, he stopped for a moment and hung his head, his chin resting on his chest as he said a quick prayer of thanks that Natalie didn't know what he had done. He had fought an inner demon all day to get his mind off Natalie and how she had looked that other morning in the thin pink nightgown and get it back on the report that was being discussed.

The problem was that, regardless of how hard he tried, his mind kept returning to the image of her pale skin and what it might feel like to touch. He had even imagined her opening her eyes, reaching up, and pulling him down to kiss her.

He unlocked the french doors and stepped out into the dusk, pausing to close his eyes and breathe deep the sultry dampness that had become familiar since he had moved close to the river.

He stood near the railing, looking out over the front yard and driveway, letting the breeze flutter through his hair to cool him. He loved this time of day when things were settling down and the night sounds took over. Even now he could hear an owl hooting. Was the owl lonely? He wasn't sure why he was allowing Natalie to affect him so much, but he knew that having her in the house was turning his well-ordered life upside down.

There was an upside to the upheaval. He liked the fact that Kelsey was happier, but all she talked about was Chester and Miss Natalie. In the eyes of the child, the tutor walked on water. In fact, he wondered if it was healthy for her to be so attached to the teacher. What if Natalie left? Kelsey would be heartbroken and it would be his fault for allowing it to continue. But what could he do?

Kelsey was doing so much better and it certainly wouldn't be fair to fire the teacher just because she was good and accomplishing more in a couple weeks than others did in months. Getting rid of the one who was responsible for the improvement was like shooting the messenger for doing her job.

He heard the french doors open behind him. With his thoughts on Natalie, he turned with a smile already forming.

"Will there be anything else this evening, sir?"

"No, Andrew, nothing else." The disappointment was immediate.

When the butler turned to leave, Trenton called out. "Wait. Andrew, could you come out here for a moment and answer a couple of questions?"

"Certainly, sir," he said, stepping out on the balcony and standing near the door, his hands crossed in front of him as he waited patiently, his face characteristically blank.

"I'm having a problem and I don't know what to do about it.

Andrew waited without interrupting. He had known Trenton for many years and knew he would say what was on his mind when he got ready.

"How long have you been working for me?" Trenton knew the answer, he just wanted it verified and he needed more time to gather his thoughts.

"Over eight years, sir."

"Yes." He stood looking out across the lawns toward the trees that loomed dark as the sun disappeared behind the horizon, signaling another day was over.

"As you know, I dated very few women before I married Kelsey's mother, but they were all cut from the same bolt of cloth." He turned to glance at the older man before resuming his perusal of the grounds, his hands reaching up to lean against the railing.

"Yes, sir, they were. If I may say so, it was like they were all twins, or maybe just went to the same finishing school."

"Exactly," he said softly, his eyes still directed to the hills. "But this one is different. She's very intelligent, yet she's simple. You know what I mean?"

"Yes sir. I think the word you're looking for is *honest*. She's not devious; she's not looking for anything except to do a good job. I believe the Americans have a saying, 'What you see is what you get.' "

"That's right," he smiled, turning to face Andrew. "There's no pretense. She's not sophisticated and phony. I think that's what I like so much about her," he admitted turning back to stare off into the growing night. "Oh, one last thing," he tossed over his shoulder. "I'm bringing a guest home for dinner tomorrow. Would you please tell the cook?"

"Yes, sir."

Sticking his hands back in his pockets, he wandered to the far end of the balcony to lean against a pillar and watch the sun paint the horizon brilliant reds and pinks before dipping further, pulling darkness over itself like a blanket.

Andrew slipped quietly away to allow his employer privacy to think. There was nothing more for him to say. Things were going quite nicely by themselves.

Chapter Five

"Trenton," the long-legged beauty purred, "you are so sweet to invite me to dinner, but all I've heard on the way over here is what a paragon this new tutor is." She flipped her midnight-black hair over her shoulder, fighting to hide the irritation at not being able to aim the conversation in the direction she wanted it to go.

"Jennifer, you had a deciding role in her selection, so I wanted you to know how much progress she has made with Kelsey," he smiled as they reached the porch. Before he could open the door, it swung inward silently to reveal Miss Mattie.

"Good evening, sir," she smiled briefly at Trenton, but ignored Jennifer, choosing to head toward the kitchen without another word.

Trenton stepped aside to allow his social secretary to enter before him.

"Well, that's nice, but I don't need to be thanked. The decision was approved by your assistant, so I can't take all the credit," she preened, her slender fingers resting on the sleeve of his jacket for a moment before she turned toward the living room. She had always loved the comfort and class that this home projected. She would have no problem giving up her townhouse for this. She'd probably keep her place as a rental. It would be nice to have a little extra income that no one else could touch.

"Daddy!" Kelsey entered the room like a whirlwind, drawing a smile from her father and a frown from Jennifer.

"Ah, my little princess. How was your day?" He gathered the little girl in his arms, cuddling her close before kissing her cheek and sitting her back on her feet.

"Great! We went over to the lake and watched a man catch a fish and then we went into town and looked at vegetables and fruits and I learned how to pick out a good watermelon," she stated, pushing out her chest in triumph.

"Fantastic," he smiled down at the little girl. "I love watermelon. Kelsey, please say hello to our guest," he instructed.

The child glanced over at the woman, but didn't turn to face her. She ducked her head and forced out a mumbled, "Hello."

Jennifer could tell that the child didn't like her, but that didn't matter. After she married Trenton, they would just send the little girl to a boarding school. Problem solved. "Hello, my dear." She looked down her nose at the child, not bothering to waste time trying to get the child to like her.

"Kel, is Miss Natalie coming down soon?"

"Yes," she beamed. "She's running behind a few minutes since she got me ready first. She'll be right down." Trenton felt Kelsey move in beside him and take his hand. Her little hand clutched tightly, her body leaning against his side. He knew Kelsey was uncomfortable around the secretary, but she was going to have to learn to deal politely with people, even if she didn't care for them.

Kelsey watched Jennifer out of the corner of her eye, but refused to look directly at her or speak to her. Trenton noticed the secretary frown at the child and wondered if the child sensed Jennifer's disapproval. He doubted the woman had spent much time around children.

"Trenton, there's no reason to bring her down to meet me since we've already met," she told him, her softly spoken words of instruction bouncing off without hitting their target.

"Nonsense. She's dining with us, so we're waiting on her. Would you care for a drink while we wait?"

"She's dining *with* us? At our table?"

Trenton looked up from watching Kelsey—drawing

a pattern on the back of his hand with her fingernail—to stare across the room at the woman who was questioning him. Until now he had assumed Jennifer was just uncomfortable around children. With her head back, she looked down her nose like he was asking her to dine with unwashed street people.

"Yes, is that a problem?" He was now tense, waiting for her answer. His parents had raised him to have much the same attitude about servants and "their place" but then they had been the servants. They had led humble lives, serving others, but hating it.

There would always be the rich and the poor, owners and servants, but he refused to allow discrimination in his home. He didn't want his daughter to learn that trait. Anyone working for him was welcome at his table even though they chose to eat in the kitchen except on rare occasions.

"Well," she said, gracefully rising to slowly make her way over to him. She took his other hand and gently squeezed as she gazed up into his eyes. "I just thought she would be uncomfortable eating with us and might be happier dining with Kelsey," she finished, her eyelashes fluttering as she smiled. Her perfume was subtle, but he preferred the musky scent that had lingered in his mind as he drifted to sleep the night before.

"She will be dining with Kelsey . . . and the two of us." His voice had become firm, daring her to continue the conversation. He admired her efficiency at the office, depended on her to do her job without a lot of input from him, even putting up with her almost constant flirtation, but he was seeing another side of her this evening—a side he wasn't sure he liked.

Natalie stopped just outside the door, out of view, as she listened to the last two statements. She had been excited to see Jennifer again. She wanted to thank her for the recommendation and the job, but now she wasn't sure of her reception. Thank goodness she knew how Trenton felt. Without that, she might have turned around and gone back upstairs. The maid could have apologized for her.

As it was, she felt off balance, unsure of the reception she would get. With a couple fortifying deep breaths, she felt confident that she was prepared to face whatever the evening held. Her mother had always told her to walk with confidence and keep her mouth closed and no one would know that she was frightened. Well, she wasn't frightened of Jennifer, but it was obvious the woman didn't want her or Kelsey around. Thank goodness the woman didn't pay the bills or make the decisions. Natalie squared her shoulders and stepped around the corner into the room.

"Good evening."

"Miss Natalie," the child left her father and rushed to grab her teacher's hand. Natalie was glad for the anchor to hold on to in the rocky waters of the hostile glare being hurled in her direction.

"What are you doing here?" Before Jennifer could stop herself, she had blurted out her question. Instantly she pulled herself back, plastered on a faint smile, and nodded toward Natalie. Despite the apparently friendly smile, her eyes gave Natalie a glimpse into her soul.

"Is there a problem?" Trenton was confused. Jennifer was the one who had told his assistant which of the final two candidates would be hired, yet now she was glaring at Natalie and asking her why she was here? None of this was making any sense at all.

Jennifer was struggling to contain her anger and restore her poise. "It seems there has been a terrible mistake. I distinctly told your assistant to hire the woman who is forty-five and has years of experience. This woman has been hired under false pretenses." Jennifer pulled her shoulders back and stiffened her spine, her nose rising an inch as she gave Natalie a dismissive look. Turning to step back to the sofa and lower herself against the pillows, she flicked her fingers toward Natalie.

"She'll just have to be replaced. This will never do."

"What are you—" His question was cut off when the maid stepped to the door to tell them that dinner was served in the dining room. Without waiting for a response, the maid returned to the kitchen to tell the staff about the four shell-shocked faces in the living room and how quiet it had been after she announced the meal.

The meal progressed with only polite conversation. Even Kelsey was muted. By the time the maid suggested serving dessert, no one was interested in sitting at the table any longer.

Natalie was at a loss as to what was going on. This

was the woman who hired her, yet she was now saying it had been a mistake and was treating her like she didn't exist. Was it only that the woman thought herself better than the hired help and didn't want to eat at the same table with her or was there something else going on? She just knew that she felt uncomfortable. She had been looking forward to the evening, but it had been ruined.

"Why don't I take Kelsey and our dessert upstairs? We can have it out on the balcony?"

Natalie had gone from pleasure as she anticipated seeing Jennifer again to shock and then to dismay. She would be fired now and have to return to West Virginia.

The worst part was that she would have to leave Kelsey, whom she had quickly grown to love. She tried not to linger on the thought of having to leave the house and Trenton. She had quickly formed feelings for him also, but she didn't want to think about that right now. She didn't want to think about never being near him again. She hesitated to admit how deep her feelings for the man might be, especially since she had seen him and the secretary sit close together at the table and keep up a flow of polite conversation. This might very well be her last evening with Kelsey. Only the decision to help Kelsey through this rough time had kept her from excusing herself and retreating to her room where she could allow herself to cry.

"Yes, that might be best. I'll be up in a bit to tuck her into bed," he said, motioning for Kelsey to come over to his chair. He knew how uncomfortable the evening had been for the child, but she had handled it with grace and he wanted her to know how proud he was of her and how much he appreciated it.

When Kelsey stepped up to his side, he wrapped his arm around her tiny waist and leaned in close to whisper.

"Thank you for being so grown up this evening and don't worry. Everything will work out," he finished before pulling her closer to kiss her cheek.

"Okay," she mumbled, leaving the room beside Natalie with her head down.

When they reached the stairs, the child broke the uncomfortable silence. "Miss Natalie, I don't want you to leave," Kelsey said, holding on to her tutor's hand and gazing up into her eyes with tears already overflowing.

"Shhh, don't worry, sweetie." She stopped to stoop down and look into the devastated eyes of the child. "I'm sure everything will work out fine," she said, trying to reassure herself as well as the child. Natalie pulled her close, rubbing her hand up and down the small back.

"That's what Daddy said." Her words were muffled against the silky smoothness of the blouse Natalie had worn with her navy silk suit.

She had worn her best outfit tonight—the one purchased for her interview—but it hadn't helped her have confidence during dinner like it had during the interview. She'd probably never wear it again. It would be too much of a reminder of this disaster in her life.

"Daddy can't fire you," she leaned back to look into

Natalie's eyes. "I love you and I'm learning how to be good since you came," she pouted, her bottom lip protruding. "It's not fair. I didn't get to vote," she stated, drawing a smile from Natalie.

"Well, dear, just for the record, neither did I." She smiled down at the child, caressing the curls and stroking her head, taking time to calm herself as well as Kelsey before the maid brought up the desserts.

"Listen," she said, pulling back so she could look directly into the child's eyes. "I'm sure this will all be settled in the morning and everything will work out, so why don't we take our desserts and milk out onto the balcony and sit at the little table and enjoy the evening? We'll worry about tomorrow later, okay?"

"Okay," she mumbled on a sigh. She pulled away from Natalie and dragged herself down the hall and out the double doors. Natalie understood her feelings perfectly. She didn't really want to go outside and eat chocolate cake. What she wanted to do was curl up in her bedroom and cry. Then she wanted to take Jennifer outside and pound on her.

When Trenton was sure he had given his daughter and Natalie sufficient time to be upstairs, he turned on Jennifer.

"I don't appreciate you being rude to Natalie in my home." He stood and glared down at Jennifer, who sat at the table with her mouth hanging open. "She works for me and you treated her with less respect than you would a bum. Have you forgotten that you're an employee of mine the same as she is?" His eyes were flashing, barely able to keep his temper under control, as he slid the chair back and stalked from the table, leaving her to follow if she wished.

His comment chilled Jennifer to the bone, but the more she thought about it, it filled her with rage. How could he compare her to the unsophisticated little tutor from the backwaters of West Virginia? Well, she'd get rid of the tutor one way or another.

It took a few moments for Jennifer to pull herself together and make her way to the living room, where Trenton was standing at the sideboard pouring a brandy. Even though she didn't like to see him irritated, she couldn't help but admire how he looked when he was angry. His eyes flashed and his nostrils flared like a wild stallion defending his turf. She felt herself grow warm with anticipation for where the evening could lead. She would just have to handle him gently.

"Would you please pour one for me? I think we've had a little misunderstanding, and I'd like for us to talk so it can get straightened out," she spoke softly, managing to sound slightly hurt.

"I'm not sure there's anything else to be said tonight," he told her without turning around, even as he picked up another glass and poured an inch of amber liquid inside it.

She arranged her body expertly in the corner of the beige sofa, allowing her slender-cut skirt to ride up a few inches on her thigh. She reached for the snifter when he approached her, allowing her fingertips to brush against his as he handed her the drink. She had just the right smile on her face as she settled in for the battle—a battle she intended to win.

Natalie had just gotten Kelsey into bed after two stories and a drink of water when she heard the bedroom door open.

"Kelsey, I wanted to say goodnight."

The child was listless as she sat up, raising her arms as her father sat on the edge of the bed. "I don't want you to fire Miss Natalie. I like her and I want her to stay," was mumbled into his neck as his large hand held her close.

"I know you do, and so do I." The little girl jerked back, staring into his eyes for confirmation. "Yippee!" she yelled, hugging her father's neck again. "She can keep on riding Juniper with me and Chester and we can all be happy," she announced.

"Now, you settle down and get to sleep. I don't want you falling asleep in the saddle tomorrow during your lesson," he smiled at his daughter as he laid her back and tucked the blanket across her chest. She looked so much like her mother. He was just happy that she didn't have her mother's disposition.

"I won't fall asleep," she giggled. "Good night." She rose on her elbow just as he reached the door. It never hurt to press your luck once in awhile. "Daddy, can we have blueberry pancakes for breakfast tomorrow?"

He stood for a moment just to look at her before answering. When he smiled Kelsey's face lit up, her smile reaching her eyes to make them sparkle once again. *Mercenary little beggar*, he thought. "I'll ask the cook if we have blueberries," he promised.

She flopped back against the pillow, pulling her doll over to tuck under the blanket with her. She smiled to herself as she saw her father crook his finger at Miss Natalie, telling her to follow him outside. This was working out just as she had hoped.

"You wanted to speak to me?" Natalie wasn't sure what she expected, but she was relieved that he had told Kelsey that she wasn't going to be fired.

"Yes, I want to apologize for the rudeness that went on downstairs. There was definitely a misunderstanding, but it wasn't the one that Miss Jennifer thought."

Natalie waited patiently as he cleared his throat and started slowly strolling down toward the balcony, indicating that she should walk with him.

"It seems that you and an older lady with the first name of Nadine were the two finalists. Jennifer must have gotten your names mixed up because she told my assistant to hire Natalie when she intended to hire Nadine."

When she remained silent, he continued. "Anyway, it was a mistake, but no harm done. I'm very pleased with what you have accomplished during the short time you've been here, so you'll be staying. I guess fate has a way of working things out the way they're supposed to be, don't you agree?"

"Yes, and thank you for the vote of confidence," she gave him a quick smile. "Well, if that's all, I think I'll head to bed."

"Actually, I have a question for you." She stopped and waited. "Am I to understand that you're still taking riding lessons?"

"Yes, is that a problem?"

"No, not at all. I guess I'm just surprised since I said you didn't have to any longer and you were . . . well, you had sore muscles and all," he hesitated slightly.

"Mr. Lancaster, I'm not a quitter." She met his eyes, gazing directly into their dark depths for several seconds. She pulled out of her trance, clearing her throat before continuing. "You and I made a deal. I would learn to ride and you would allow Kelsey to take lessons. I don't feel that managing to not fall off the animal would be considered learning to ride, wouldn't you agree?"

"Well, my hat's off to you. I commend you for not only taking the challenge in the first place, but to being willing to carry it through to its conclusion," he said, bowing slightly at the waist.

"Well, thank you, kind sir and may you have a good night's sleep," she curtsied before her soft laughter rose to blend with the sounds of the water splashing in the fountain just below them.

"Good night. See you in the morning. Be prepared for blueberry pancakes," he warned, a smile tickling the corners of his eyes.

"Oh? Is there a reason that it's a warning?"

"Just be forewarned that my daughter will request blueberry pancakes at any and all occasions. Birthdays, anniversaries, and any occasion when she thinks she has the upper hand and might be able to wiggle them out of me as a prize or a reward. So, if you don't like blueberry pancakes, you might either learn to like them or bribe the cook for some eggs," he said, a chuckle taking his face from somber and serious to a radiant smile.

"Oh, I see. Then I guess it's a good thing I like them. Well, good night, again." She stepped into the hallway, closing the french doors behind her to keep insects from entering the house.

He felt as if he had just shed ten pounds. She had a way of making him feel younger and more carefree. Even though he dealt with serious matters all day, he felt like he was getting out of school for the summer every evening when he left for home.

Trenton moved to the railing and stood looking down at the gardens and the fountain below. Small path lights dotted the landscape, giving the grounds below a mystical, enchanted look. He knew it was unusual for him to think of whimsical things, but it had suddenly become a magical night.

Chapter Six

Jennifer poured over the application that Natalie had sent in to the agency. She reread the letters of recommendation sent in from her professor and her clergyman. She looked at her transcript, frowning as she realized that Natalie's grades were far superior to her own.

"I must have missed something. There has to be something on here that she lied about. There has to be something . . ." She snapped her fingers. She sat pondering for several seconds before a smile slowly spread across her face. "It doesn't have to be academics. It can be trustworthiness and that can't be recorded on a transcript."

Her smile turned devious as her mind whirled with the possibility of discrediting the lofty Miss Natalie. She leaned back in the swivel chair, her head thrown back and her eyes closed as she pondered her options.

All she had to do was figure out what angle she could use to bring down the paragon of virtue.

With renewed energy and enthusiasm, she hunched over the file laying open on her desk, starting again at the top to read slowly, analyzing every entry. She would find what she needed if it took her all day.

"Daddy, it's Saturday, and you don't have to go to the office, so would you go riding with me and Miss Natalie? Mr. Clyde says I'm getting quite good and he's very proud of me," she ended, her fork now poised over her pancake while she looked hopefully at her father.

He took the time to drain his coffee cup before he answered her. He sat for a couple moments just staring at his daughter, but wondering if being with Natalie all morning was a good idea. He didn't need any more distractions right now when the United Nations was gearing up for a vote on possible sanctions on some countries that were harboring terrorists. He was already spending too much time thinking about the woman. He even dreamed about her last night, and she was the first thing on his mind when he woke up this morning. Natalie and her blasted pink nightgown were getting him off track.

"Daddy?" she prompted.

He didn't have the heart to turn her down. She had been working so hard to learn how to ride Chester and how to take good care of him. He had been getting almost daily reports from Clyde and he was being told that the child was a natural. Well, that remained to be seen, but the more he thought about it, the more a ride across the pastures sounded like just the thing to do.

"All right, Kell-Bell. We'll all go for a ride. Is that okay with you, Miss Natalie?"

She sat eating her pancake in silence, hoping that he would tell the child he was too busy. She knew he had stayed up late the prior evening in his study working. It was after midnight when she got up for a drink and had seen the light on in the office. She had tiptoed past the door, not even glancing in. Right now, all she could focus on was that even the thought of riding with him made her stomach quiver.

"Natalie?" "Miss Natalie?" Father and daughter spoke in unison, pulling her out of deep thoughts.

"Oh, yes, sure. We can all go for a ride. That sounds nice," she fumbled, setting her fork down now that she had lost her appetite.

Even though she felt she was doing much better and she was no longer getting sore when she rode, she still felt embarrassed at the thought of him watching her ride. Her form wasn't what it should be and she bounced too much. Clyde was always telling her to move with the flow of the horse, but she still hadn't quite gotten the rhythm of it all.

"Yeah!" Kelsey jumped up from the table and darted from the room. "I'll get dressed," she called out over her shoulder as she stormed up the stairs.

"How do you put up with her energy every day?" He smiled, trying to ease her obvious nervousness.

She glanced toward the stairs before her eyes darted back to clash with his. "Oh, she's not a problem. I think I'll go up and help her get into her riding clothes and get myself ready. We should be down in about fifteen minutes. We'll just meet you at the stable, if you'd like," she offered.

"I'll see you when you're ready."

Trenton called ahead so the horses would be ready when they arrived. They were walking the path toward the corral, but Kelsey was impatient. She kept running ahead and then retracing her steps to encourage the couple to hurry up.

Natalie understood her excitement. Kelsey always attacked life head-on, rushing from one activity to another. Today she was in a rush to get to the stable and ride Chester and the only thing slowing her down were the two adults.

"Hurry up, you guys. The day is wasting," she admonished them.

They glanced at each other before bursting into laughter. They both knew that she had picked up the saying from Clyde. He was always hurrying them along when it was time to get in the saddle and get on with the lesson.

"You know, Kels, it's not necessarily a bad thing to take your time and walk through life smelling the roses," Natalie told the child.

"Huh?" She scrunched up her face in question.

"She means that sometimes it's good to take your time

and enjoy yourself as you go, not just rush through life and then wonder where all the years went," he said to clarify, his eyes connected with Natalie's.

"Huh? You guys aren't making any sense. I'm in a hurry because I want to go riding. I don't want to smell flowers," she finished emphatically.

By silent agreement they decided to drop the subject and just try to enjoy the day.

Clyde helped Natalie into the saddle while Trenton helped his daughter.

"Is everyone ready?" When he got a nod from Natalie and a loud "Yes, sir" from Kelsey, he lead the girls through the gate and into the pasture at a walking pace.

"Isn't this fun? We can all ride, just like a family," the child said, her face sporting a smile that spread from ear to ear. Neither adult missed the comment.

Natalie could feel her face growing warm. It was so obvious what the child wanted, but that wasn't possible. She had nothing in common with Trenton, not to mention that he was her employer. Besides, from the way Jennifer had looked at Trenton, the woman was either his girlfriend or had plans in that direction.

She knew she was no match for Jennifer's sophistication. She hated to disappoint the child, but Kelsey would eventually have to realize that she couldn't have everything she wanted in life. Her heart was hurting as she concentrated on her form.

They walked the horses for almost fifteen minutes before reaching the trail leading into the woods. They were riding three abreast, but the path was becoming narrower and by necessity, they formed a single line through the trees.

"Natalie, do you want to lead the way and I'll bring up the rear?"

"Okay." She nudged the horse in the side, trotting forward a few feet before settling back down to a loping walk.

"Kelsey, keep your knees in tighter and your back a little straighter," called out her father.

Even though he had been talking to Kelsey, Natalie checked the position of her knees and straightened her back. She loved riding through the woods. It was cooler and she loved the smells. It reminded her of back home on The Hill. She had been in such a hurry to leave; yet, every time she turned around, she was reminded of home.

"Hey, Natalie," he called out. "You're doing really well for a beginner. Before long Clyde will have you galloping across the meadows," he chuckled as he watched her rump bounce up and down in the saddle. She was wearing a pair of faded Levi jeans and tennis shoes. He'd have to take her shopping to get the proper pants and a pair of boots. In fact, he noted, he needed to get the proper clothing for Kelsey as well.

An hour later they arrived back at the stable, tired but happy as they left the horses for Clyde and Andrew to take care of while they walked toward home.

Nearing the house, they heard a car coming up the

road. When it popped over the hill, Trenton saw that it was Jennifer's Mustang.

"What does she want?" Kelsey had yet to learn the art of tact and diplomacy. She still said exactly what came into her head. "I don't like her," she mumbled, lowering her chin and glaring toward the car racing up the drive.

"Kelsey, you'll be polite to our guests, whether you care for them or not," her father admonished.

Kelsey ran for the house, darting up the steps and inside before the car came to a stop in front of the water fountain. Natalie wished she could also run away, but manners stopped her. She would smile and act like the lady her mother had tried to raise, even if the smile split her face in two and the words she wanted to say slid down her throat and choked her.

They stood waiting at the foot of the steps while Jennifer slid her legs from the car and walked toward them. She was wearing a white linen pantsuit that looked tailored to fit every curve perfectly. Her make-up was the perfect foil to the ebony hair that swung down loose just below her shoulders.

She had eyes only for Trenton as she made her way over to where they waited. She had a leather purse hanging over one shoulder and a briefcase clutched in her left hand that sported a huge diamond solitaire nested amid several opals. The ring was exquisite.

Natalie was momentarily stunned. Was that an engagement ring? Natalie didn't think she had ever heard that the woman was engaged. Maybe she had been wrong about Jennifer wanting to marry the ambassador. Still, next to the woman who looked like she had shown up for a photo shoot, Natalie felt frumpy. Her hair was coming out of the ponytail, she had long since sweated off the little bit of make-up she had put on that morning, and her clothes were old, faded, and sweaty.

"Hi, Jennifer. What brings you out here today?"

Trenton gave her a pleasant smile, only his clinched jaw showed his irritation. It had taken only a short time for Natalie to learn the sign. It reminded her of her grandfather. The male role model in her life had rarely shown outward emotion, only the subtle impressions that she had learned to recognize.

"I'm sorry," she smiled. "Did I interrupt anything?" She ran her eyes from Natalie's head down to her feet and back up to smile like a cat that had just been handed a bowl of milk. "I had a few things I wanted to go over with you about next month's charity dinner at the club."

"If you'll excuse me, I'll change," Natalie said, not waiting for an answer. She was seething by the time she topped the stairs and entered her bedroom, wanting to slam the door, but quietly shutting it in case the couple had come inside. She wouldn't give that woman the satisfaction of knowing how inferior she had felt beside her.

She took a quick shower, washed her hair, and then sat on the stool in front of the mirror to blow it dry. She lowered her arm for a moment to stare at her face. Why was she still single at almost thirty? Her mother had told her on numerous occasions that she was too picky. Natalie chose to think of herself as discerning.

She didn't think she was ugly. In fact, she thought she was rather attractive. She had large deep blue eyes and every man she had ever dated had commented on them, but she liked her smile the best. No orthodontist had been needed to achieve the straight white teeth.

"Thanks mom," she whispered, smiling at herself in the mirror. Her complexion was clear and smooth with just a hint of sun giving a pink glow to her cheeks. All in all, she had good features. She just needed to remember that when Jennifer was around.

The more she thought about Jennifer, the angrier she got with herself for allowing the woman to make her feel small and ugly. She knew better, so all she had to do was ignore the woman and focus on taking care of Kelsey.

It still galled her that Trenton couldn't see what the woman was really like, but if he wanted to work with a shrew, then that was his choice. It was none of her business as long as Kelsey was well taken care of. She hoped the woman was engaged to another man and didn't have her eyes on Trenton. Even the thought of Trenton with that woman made her stomach muscles tighten, but it also hurt to think of a woman like Jennifer as a mother for Kelsey. It would be disastrous for the child.

She could tell that Kelsey didn't like Jennifer and the part that made her the saddest was that she could tell Jennifer didn't care one hoot about the child. All she seemed to care about was Trenton. Well, if he wanted her, then he could have her—as his assistant or as his wife. If he was that blind and if he wanted her type of sophistication and glamour, then he could just have her. It was his choice.

"If they get married, I'll even dance at their wedding," she muttered, tugging on her wet hair as she brushed out the tangles.

She lowered the brush she was using on her hair. Dance at their wedding? In a pig's eye. There would be a cold day in hell when she celebrated them getting married.

Chapter Seven

Natalie was thankful that Jennifer had not stayed for dinner. Whatever her reason for leaving, at least it would be a peaceful evening. Even Kelsey was in a good mood as they sat playing Go Fish at the card table that had been set up in the living room.

"Do you have any twos?"

"Go fish," Natalie told the child.

When she turned to Trenton, she narrowed her eyes and glanced down at the sizable collection of cards he held in his hand. His luck wasn't going very well, so far.

"Do you have any aces?"

"Oh darn," Trenton mumbled as he handed over the two cards and Natalie laid her three cards down to "go out."

"You won!" Kelsey squealed, bouncing up and down on her chair.

"Well, that makes a game for each of you two ladies. I think my luck is gone. Why don't we call it a night and get some sleep?"

Kelsey immediately started to protest when her father held up his hand. "Wait a minute, I didn't have a chance to finish. After church tomorrow, why don't we drive over to the city? I have three tickets to see *Lion King* at the afternoon showing in the theater."

"You mean we can go to a Broadway play?" Kelsey was already out of the chair and over hugging her father's neck. "Thank you, thank you, thank you! I've always wanted to go see one. This is so super." She danced around in circles, her arms out like a ballerina. She came to a sudden stop. "Miss Natalie, what should I wear?"

"Let's go upstairs and take a look in your closet," she suggested. As she stood, Kelsey was already grabbing for her hand to drag her upstairs. When they got to the door of the living room, Natalie looked over her shoulder and mouthed, "thank you" before turning her attention to the excited child.

It took another two hours for Kelsey to pick out a dress for the next day, take a bath, and get settled into bed. By then Natalie was exhausted yet restless, and unable to settle down. She knew she would have a difficult time getting to sleep if she went to bed, so she grabbed her bathrobe and headed down the hall to the balcony.

She was gazing up at the Big Dipper when she heard the door open behind her. It made her flinch, but almost instantly she smelled his aftershave. Her heart thudded, her jaw clamped, and she sucked in and held her breath.

"Hi. Did I disturb you?"

Her breath whooshed out as she glanced over her shoulder to smile at him. "No, I just couldn't relax so I came out for a few minutes to enjoy the stars. I love being outside at night," she smiled at him as he walked over and stood alongside her, leaning over to rest his arms on top of the railing. He clasped his hands together and gazed upward.

"When I stand outside at night and look up into the heavens, I feel so small down here," he admitted. "When I was a boy, I used to imagine going into space in a rocket ship or living in the space station. It all seemed so exciting then. Now, I think I'd die of boredom."

"Well, just think. There's men out there right now on the space station and they're staring at Earth from up there saying that they'd hate to be on Earth with all it's traffic and pollution and how happy they are to be there." She smiled into the dark.

"Yeah, you're probably right. We don't always think about things from the other guy's point of view. We should each be happy about our lot in life and make the most of it, right?"

"Well, not necessarily," she chuckled. "If I had taken that advice, I'd not be Kelsey's tutor right now."

"What do you mean?"

"Well, I was born in a poor area of West Virginia to poor parents. When my father was killed, my mother moved back with her parents so they could help her raise my three brothers and myself. If I had accepted where I came from I'd still be back there, like the rest of my family. I'm the only one who went to college and I'm the only one who has gotten off the mountain. I was never content with my lot in life. I always wanted more," she admitted. "I always felt that I could have whatever I was willing to work for."

She was surprised at herself for telling him about her family. Even though it was all in her file somewhere, she seldom told anyone about her background. She didn't want anyone to look down on her, like Jennifer did, and she didn't want anyone feeling sorry for her. She couldn't see Trenton's face, so she didn't know what his reaction was to her story.

"Well, I have to admire your guts. I would imagine that you had to work hard to get yourself out of the environment you were raised in. You had to break out of small-town thinking."

"Also small-person thinking. I was always told that I'd never amount to anything and never have all the things I wanted in life. I was told that my head was always in the clouds and my eyes were always on the stars." She laughed out loud as she waved her arms out in an arc toward the sky. "Well, I guess they were right. I still have my eyes on the stars."

He turned his head at the sound of her laughter. The moon was shining enough for him to see her face, to know that her eyes were sparkling and she was happy. He had missed having someone to talk with at the end of the day. He missed having someone to share feelings and discuss Kelsey with. He missed having someone to sleep in his arms at night and to give him a hug and a kiss when he came home in the evening. He missed having a wife.

He lifted a hand to tuck a stray wisp of hair behind her ear. As she turned to look at him, he moved the short distance to stand, gently pulling her toward him. He hesitated only a moment to stare down into her large eyes before leaning over and lightly touching his lips to hers. When she didn't pull away, he deepened the kiss, gathering her closer and then still closer.

Her arms slowly reached up to drape around his neck, her lips opening to his touch. She felt a tingle jet through her body from her scalp down to her toes. When he started pulling away she moaned inwardly, feeling adrift, lost in a sea of emotions that swirled around in her head, drugging her mind, making her limp, wanting the kiss to never stop.

"Natalie, I'm sorry, I didn't mean to do this. I shouldn't have kissed you. You work for me and I don't . . ." He ran his hand through his hair and turned his back on her, standing with his head bent.

Natalie was devastated. She had been floating on one of the fleecy clouds that were drifting overhead between them and the millions of stars, and he had just knocked her off to plummet to the ground with a resounding thud.

She had grabbed at what she wanted, held it in her hands for one blissful moment, and suddenly it had become mist to disappear on the breeze. There was no substance to what had just happened, at least not on Trenton's side. He was probably feeling guilty for letting the moon and stars get to him.

Without another word she turned and rushed through the doors, down the hall and into her room without looking back and with no delusions about what had just happened. She had allowed him to kiss her, had kissed him back even, and now she was going to have to swallow her pride and face him in the morning, knowing that he felt nothing for her even if she was falling in love with him.

"Damn," she muttered as she remembered that they were scheduled to spend the entire next day together. Well, she'd smile and make the best of it. She refused to ruin Kelsey's outing. She would get through this one day at a time until she could get her emotions, her feelings for the man, under control. No matter how long it took. And it might take a very, very long time.

The day had gone better than she had expected. She had been nervous about seeing him after the kiss the evening before, but he had acted normal, like nothing had happened between them. There was an odd ache in her chest. Her heart felt heavy.

Natalie mentally shook herself. If that was the way he wanted to handle it, then that was fine with her. Actually, she thought, pulling back her shoulders and holding her head higher, it took some of the pressure off.

But it also hurt that he could dismiss their kiss so easily. That kiss had kept her awake for most of the night. She would just have to accept that it hadn't meant anything to him. It had just been the atmosphere—the stars and moonlight—and she had been the one available. It meant nothing to him.

"Are we almost home? I want to play my CD. I just loved all the music." Kelsey didn't even wait for an answer before she was off again on how wonderful the play had been.

It had been a delight to see Kelsey's eyes light up as she sat on the edge of her seat during the stage performance. It had been Natalie's first Broadway show as well and she had been just as mesmerized. The dancers and the music had been almost overwhelming, but now the show was over and she was back on Earth.

"Daddy, can we go to another play sometime? I think I want to be a dancer on stage someday. I love the clothes and the band."

"Yes, someday when another good show arrives, we'll go again." He smiled down at his daughter as she continued to chatter. When he glanced up at Natalie, she was staring at him, but the instant he smiled, she jerked her gaze to the scenery flipping by.

He had watched her during the performance. She had been enthralled, the same as Kelsey. He loved watching both of them, but the magic seemed to have faded from Natalie's eyes. They were now empty, sad, even haunted. Was she thinking about the play? Or her life here with Kelsey and himself?

They pulled up in front of the house, directly behind a muddy Land Rover.

"Sir, were you expecting company?" Andrew had lowered the window between them when he spotted the vehicle.

Trenton glanced out the window, but had no clue who was at the house.

"No. Everyone stay in the car until I can check it out. Lock up behind me," he instructed.

He stepped out, but had only gotten to the bottom of the steps when a man stepped out on the porch.

"Well, well, well. The wayward have returned home at last," the man said, chuckling as he walked forward.

Trenton stopped with one foot on the bottom step, staring up at the man he had never seen before. He turned around when he heard Natalie's voice behind him. She had just stepped out of the car and was running toward the house.

"John?" She breezed past Trenton as the man came down the steps, both of them laughing. As they reached each other, the man's arms went around her, lifting her off the ground to swing her around in a circle.

"Why are you here? When did you get here? How long can you stay?" Her rapid-fire questions were intermixed with laughter when he finally sat her down, but didn't relinquish his hold on her.

"I'm so excited to see you," she said, leaning in to give him a tight hug. Only then did she start to take stock of her brother's appearance. He had no doubt been hunting and his flannel shirt and dirty jeans were wrinkled and a thick dark beard, sprinkled with a few gray whiskers, covered his face. Now that she thought about it, he had body odor. He probably hadn't showered since he left West Virginia, and there was no telling how long he had been out in the woods.

She pulled back and turned toward Trenton, forcing herself to take a breath and calm down before making the introductions. Kelsey had come up beside her father and was tucked close beside him, his hand resting protectively on her shoulder.

"Trenton, Kelsey, I'd like you both to meet my oldest brother, John."

She saw an immediate change in both faces as they smiled, Trenton stepping forward to shake hands with the rough-looking man still holding Natalie close to his side.

"Nice to meet you both. You taking care of my kid sister here?" He squeezed her shoulders, his possessiveness beginning to embarrass her. She pulled away and turned toward the house.

"Actually, she's helping to take care of us," Trenton grinned. "This is my daughter, Kelsey. Natalie is her tutor," he supplied.

"Well, ain't that special?" he sneered, standing a little taller, but still managing to be several inches shorter than Trenton.

Natalie could feel the tension starting to build. "Come on, let's get out of this heat. Would everyone like a cool drink?"

"Yeah, I'll have a beer. Nothing better than a cold brew on a hot day to cool a man's throat."

Natalie gave her brother a stern look as she took Kelsey by the hand and led her into the house, the two men trailing behind.

"Make that two beers, Natalie," Trenton said as they reached the porch and he held the door for everyone to walk inside. She started toward the kitchen, with Kelsey still in tow. She would make sure that Kelsey was around her crude brother as little as possible. Behind her she heard Trenton take over the conversation.

"So, you're Natalie's brother. Are you visiting in the area?" Natalie had to commend Trenton for trying to be hospitable. She wished she could slide under one of the rare Persian rugs that dotted the wood floors or maybe dry up and blow away on the wind. It wasn't that she was embarrassed about her background, exactly, but it was so obvious that John had no class, no tact when dealing in an unfamiliar environment. She felt badly for him. She was sure he was uncomfortable.

"Miss Natalie, is that really your brother?" Her eyes were huge as she stared up at her teacher.

"Yes." She smiled down at the little girl. "He's quite a few years older than me." She passed the information about refreshments along to a maid before asking the other maid to take Kelsey and her juice upstairs and keep her busy until dinner. She wanted to get back to the living room as quickly as possible. She had no idea what outrageous things John might say and she wanted to be there as a buffer.

The men were in earnest conversation when she got back. As she could have imagined, they were discussing hunting. That was her brother's one passion and it consumed most of his life, as well as most of his money.

"Yeah, I'm on my way back from Idaho, heading home. I got one trophy set of horns, but the pickings were slim. I don't shoot anything unless it's got a good rack," he bragged. When he saw her come back into the room, his gaze dropped to her empty hands just before he frowned. She rushed to explain before he said anything.

"The maid will bring the drinks in just a moment," she smiled.

"The maid, huh? Yeah, I got me one of those. Been married to her for fifteen years," he joked, his belly laugh resounding off the walls of the professionally decorated room. She sat on the winged-back chair, hovering near the edge so she could react quickly if necessary.

"Natalie, please relax. We're having a very enjoyable conversation." Trenton smiled before turning back to the man slouched in the corner of the sofa. "So, John, you said you were in Idaho and on your way back home. How long can you stay with us?"

"Stay here?" He took a few seconds to scan the room before he spoke. It was obvious he had never stayed in a home the size or the quality of this one, but the smile he gave Trenton could only be described as humorous.

"Can't say that I've ever stayed in a place like this. I got my camping gear with me, but it might be interesting to sleep in one of these"—he indicated the entire house—"for a night. I've got to be on my way in the morning. Gotta get to work on Tuesday. Gotta have that paycheck, you know," he winked at Trenton before reaching for his glass of beer the maid carried in on the tray.

He sat looking at the glass for a moment before taking a long swallow, wiping foam from his top lip with the back of his hand and letting out a loud sigh. "Good stuff. What brand do you buy?"

"It's a Dunkel Lager. I import it from Europe."

"Hummm, good stuff," he said, taking another big swallow. Two swallows later the Pilsner glass was empty. She was praying he wouldn't belch. Her brothers used to have belching contests when she was younger, and John always won.

"So, how are Mom and the boys?" She was uncomfortable and couldn't believe Trenton had asked him to stay the night. She held her glass of cola, rattling the ice but not drinking. The glass just gave her something to do with her hands.

"Oh, she's okay. Just getting old is all. She can't get around like she used to so Brenda goes over to help her with the laundry and such. We've been talking about moving back to the hill to live there and take care of her."

Natalie knew the real reason for the move and it had nothing to do with their mother and her health. She once overheard John tell his best friend that the brother who was in the house when their mother died would be the one to keep it. Her brother was all about money and the more he didn't have to spend on rent payments would be more that he could spend on hunting trips, card games on Friday nights, and beer. Yeah, she knew her brother all too well. He was an opportunist. She knew that in the eyes of her mother, the sun rose and set over the head of her oldest son and even though he was in it for the money, Natalie knew that John's wife loved her mother-in-law and would take good care of her.

"Natalie, would you like to take your brother up and show him to the guest room? He might want to rest a bit before dinner is served." He turned to face John as he stood. "I'm glad to meet one of Natalie's brothers and I hope you enjoy your stay with us tonight. I've got a little bit of work to do before we dine, so I'll leave you in your sister's capable hands and I'll see you at dinner." He nodded at John before leaving the room.

John stretched back to look down the hall before he spoke. "Well, little sister, you sure came out smelling like a rose. How much you getting paid to live high on the hog?"

"John," she pleaded, "would you please dredge up every manner you ever learned or ever even heard about and use them while you're here?"

"Why, baby sister, are you ashamed of me? Are you ashamed of where you come from?" He leered at her, leaning forward to slap her on the knee. "Where did you get all them highfalutin ways? Over at that big college you went to?"

She was regretting having said anything. If John thought she was putting him down, he'd probably act up on purpose and no telling what would happen or what he'd do.

"John, you know I'm not ashamed of you. If I had been, I wouldn't have given you such a big hug when I saw you. The only thing is that these people are from England and they act differently, and I just don't want to offend them. They're guests in our country." Thankfully, he seemed to buy her story.

"Well," he said, scratching his head, "I guess you're right. Don't seem right to be rude to foreigners unless they're rude to you first and this guy, Trenton, has been nice, I guess. Trenton," he laughed. "Damn sissy name, if you ask me." He chuckled as he said the name again to himself.

There was nothing she could say to him on that subject. Sometimes it was best to pick your fights, and this one wasn't worth the time or energy.

"Come on, I'll show you to your room. You might want to take a nap or a shower or something for the next hour until dinner." She was heading toward the stairs, assuming he would follow her. When she had gone up several steps and he still wasn't behind her, she stopped and waited a moment before returning to the living room.

On the far side of the room John stood in front of a glass case that held antique dueling guns and ornate knives. It was an extensive collection that she figured was worth a lot of money.

"John? Are you coming?"

"Did you see this stuff? Sissy little guns and knives. I can't imagine using them for anything." He laughed as he pointed toward a weapon in the case. "Can you imagine me shooting at a boar with that tiny little thing?"

"Those aren't for hunting. They're for dueling." When John looked confused, she continued. "When two men had a disagreement, they'd each take a gun and stand back to back and then walk away from each other for ten steps, turn and fire at one another. The best shot won. Or sometimes a gun would misfire, so the one that got a bullet fired was the one who won."

"Huh. Stupid thing to do. I'd just turn on the count of

nine and shoot the guy before he could turn around," he snickered.

That didn't surprise her one bit. "You mean you'd shoot a man in the back?"

"Sure, if it meant I wouldn't be shot," he said, matter-of-factly.

"Come on." This time he followed her up the stairs, whistling when she opened a door and indicated that the room was his.

"Well ain't this fancy," he laughed as he stood in the middle of the room and turned in a circle. He walked over to the door leading into the bathroom. "Whoa Nelly, would you look at this?" He was already examining all the fixtures and sizing up the room.

"I'm in the room to your right, so if you need any-thing, just knock on my door. I'll be resting for a bit before dinner." She stepped back out into the hall, closing the door behind her. Her eyes lifted toward heaven, sending a quick prayer that her brother would behave and not ruin the family name while he was visiting.

Once in her room, she discarded her dress and took a quick shower before slipping on a pair of tan slacks and a blouse her brother and sister-in-law had given her the past Christmas. After applying a minimum amount of makeup, she headed downstairs to see what the cook was preparing for dinner. When she was told that it was roast and mashed potatoes, she was relieved. She even took a chance in asking the cook if there was any possi-bility of getting apple pie for dessert.

"Well, ma'am, I had planned peach cobbler with ice cream. Will that do?"

"Yes, that's perfect. Thank you so much."

"Thank you, ma'am. Umm," she stammered, looking toward the floor before bringing her eyes up to meet Natalie's. "I hope I'm not speaking out of line, but I wanted to tell you that I've noticed a difference with our little Miss Kelsey since you've been here. She is so much more polite." She looked a little flustered, but smiled quickly to hide her nervousness.

"Why, thank you. That's a sweet thing to say, and I'm glad you told me." Natalie climbed the stairs without noticing, her mind on what the cook had just told her. She was so proud of Kelsey. She was such a sweet child. It was a shame that her mother was no longer here, but at least she still had a father who loved her . . . and she had a tutor who adored her.

Her steps slowed as she passed Trenton's suite doors. She wanted to see him and thank him for being gracious toward her brother, but she didn't think she could knock on his door and disturb him. She'd just have to tell him later.

She continued on down to Kelsey's door and tapped lightly. The maid opened the door with a finger to her lips. She stepped out into the hallway before speaking.

"She's taking a short nap. Should I stay with her?"

"No, that's fine. I'll take care of her now. Thank you so much for coming up with her."

The maid nodded and quickly disappeared down the

back stairs. Natalie turned toward her room when she saw Trenton's bedroom door open. They stood looking at each other for a moment before he motioned for her to come to him.

"Yes?" she whispered.

"I just want you to know that I realize the world is made up of all sorts of people and your brother is just one type," he smiled, taking her hand and running his thumb over her knuckles. "In fact—"

"Well, is this the way it goes around here?"

Natalie jerked her hand back, whirling around to face John. She hadn't heard his door open and now he stood with his hands in his pockets, laughing at her discomfort.

"Are you ready to go down to dinner?" She stared her brother straight in the eyes, daring him to say anything else. She was thankful to see that he had taken a shower and had on clean clothes, but if he embarrassed her further she would very likely forget her manners.

Her glare told him just how furious she was and how things would go down if he dared to tease her. He raised his hands like he had been caught robbing a store. "I surrender. I was only kidding." He smiled to take the edge off as he sauntered toward the couple.

Without any further conversation, the three descended the stairs to spend the evening talking about horses and hunting.

After dinner Natalie left the men smoking cigars and talking while she went upstairs to check on Kelsey. She found her in her room eating from a tray with one of her dolls sitting in one of the chairs at the small table.

"Are you all right?"

"Oh yes. Marisa and me are having a grand dinner. Afterwards, we're going to dance with handsome princes and ride home in a huge carriage pulled by white horses."

"Do you plan to be home before the clock strikes twelve times?"

"Um hum. Otherwise, I'll be walking. My carriage will turn into a pumpkin."

"Well, you seem to have that story down."

"Miss Natalie," the little girl started, staring down at her plate where she was moving her vegetables around. "Is your brother nice?"

"Yes, I'd say he's fairly nice, why?"

"Because he looks mean," she said. "He scares me," she whispered holding her tiny hand up next to her mouth like she was confiding a secret.

"Well," she smiled, "you don't have to worry about John. He has a little girl of his own and he would never hurt you. He just looks a little scary because he has been out in the woods sleeping for a few days and he needs a shave."

"Can I sleep with you tonight?"

"Well, you know what? I just might be able to get the cook to send us up some hot chocolate and peach cobbler, and we can have it sitting in the middle of my bed while we read Cinderella. How does that sound?"

"Great," she beamed.

"Then let me go downstairs and get our desserts and tell the men goodnight. You meet me in my room when I get back."

"Okay. Come on, Marisa. We have to get our things together to sleep over with Miss Natalie. She has this super big bed with lots of pillows and she wears this neat perfume," she told the doll as she grabbed her by the arm and stuck her under one arm as she headed for her bed to get her pillow.

Chapter Eight

"**H**urry, Miss Natalie, wake up," the little girl ordered, her voice holding an excited urgency that had Natalie opening her eyes.

"What is it, Munchkin?"

"I just went down to breakfast and guess what?" When Natalie didn't answer, she continued on, her voice singing out the words while she danced around the room.

"We're having pancakes. We're having pancakes." Kelsey was all smiles when she stopped twirling and again hovered near the edge of the bed.

"Come on!"

Natalie was sure the child's whine could be heard all the way down the hall.

"Okay, I'm getting up, but what's the occasion?"

"I don't know, but it's always something special when

116

I get blueberry pancakes, and this time I didn't even ask for them," she whispered.

"Well, why don't you go back downstairs and give me ten minutes to get up and dressed and then I'll be down?"

"Okay," she said, pointing one small finger toward Natalie before issuing her last order. "And don't be late. I want to find out what's going to happen." With that she turned and darted from the room, slamming the door behind her.

Natalie closed her eyes, rubbing them with one finger and thumb. "What in the world could be happening today that's special?"

It had been a week since her brother's visit and life had slid into a comfortable rut. She had never been happier and more content in her life. Or more tired. She had been up way past midnight reading a new mystery book and it had cost her several hours of sleep. She lay for another couple minutes before tossing off the blanket and getting out of bed. She glanced at the clock on her way to the bathroom. The little cherub had just cost her half an hour of sleep. God bless her little heart.

She was sure she had made it within the allotted ten minutes, but she could hear Kelsey complaining as she rounded the corner and pulled out her chair.

"You're late," Kelsey accused.

"You're lucky I'm here now, so don't press your luck." She stared at the little girl, but the slight frown didn't seem to be having much effect.

"Now that we're all here," Trenton said, "let's eat."

"But Daddy, what's the surprise?"

"Surprise? Who said there was going to be a surprise?"

"Daddy!"

"Okay," he chuckled. "Eat your breakfast and then I have something to show you and Miss Natalie."

Kelsey made quick work of her pancake, leaving most of her milk before announcing that she was finished.

"Well, you might as well sit and finish since I can't show you until Miss Natalie and I are finished also."

The child pouted, kicking her foot against the table leg as she glared at the adults who were taking their time eating. When she looked up to see her father frowning at her she stopped her foot, but slouched down in the chair to continue to pout.

When the maid came in to clear the table, Trenton stepped into the kitchen and came back with two big wrapped boxes. Kelsey's squeal could be heard throughout the house when her father handed her one of the big boxes, and the other to Natalie.

Natalie was shocked. What could he be buying for her? She was staring at him, her mouth slightly open when he started chuckling and reached over with one finger under her jaw to push her mouth closed.

"Open it, would you?"

Kelsey already had the bow off and was ripping at the paper before Natalie could even bring her thoughts into focus.

When Kelsey finally got down to the box and got the

lid off, she was speechless for several seconds before she jumped up from the table, ignoring that the box and it's contents fell to the floor, in order to run to her father and throw her arms around his neck.

"Thank you, thank you, thank you! This is what I've always wanted," she screeched before rushing back around to pick up her new riding outfit from the floor.

She was already out of the room and on her way upstairs when Trenton turned to Natalie. "Well, aren't you going to open yours?" He propped his elbows on the table while Natalie started unwrapping her box.

When she lifted the lid, she was speechless. Inside was a silk blouse and fawn colored spandex riding pants with leather leg guards on the inner thigh. On the bottom of the box was a pair of brown riding boots. She sat staring at the items in the box, trying to stop the tears that threatened to spill down her cheeks.

Her eyes glistened when she lifted them to stare at Trenton. "Thank you so much. They're beautiful. I had no idea . . . I can't imagine . . ." She took a deep breath before finishing. "I'm overwhelmed. This is too much," she said, a gentle smile touching the corners of her mouth as she reached up to wipe away a few tears.

"You deserve it," he said, reaching across to tuck a stray wisp of hair behind her ear. "You've been so good for Kelsey. She has always been a little precocious, but you have really brought her out and gotten her to widen her horizons. And for that, I thank you. You've given her courage to try some new things just by your willingness to learn the same thing at the same time. You seem to have been able to fill the void left when her mother was killed. In short, she trusts you."

"Thank you, but you didn't have to buy this for me. But I do appreciate it," she smiled.

"Well, aren't you going to go put it on so we can go riding?"

"Aren't you going into the office today?"

"No, I took the day off. It seems there is a technical glitch with my computer and they've got people coming out today to fix it. The bottom line is that they don't want me in the way."

"Then, I'll be right back," she beamed. She was as excited about having the extra time with him as she was about the outfit. She had just reached the top of the stairs when Kelsey stormed out of her room.

"Look at me! Look at me! I'm beautiful!" She twirled around, showing off her new outfit.

"Yes you are," Natalie said, gathering the child close with one arm for a quick hug. "Now, head down and give me a few minutes to change clothes. I'll hurry," she promised, using her finger to cross her heart. With the box tucked under one arm, she opened the door to her room and stepped inside.

She was still trying to get used to the idea that when she left her room in the mornings someone came in and made the bed, cleaned the bathroom and picked up anything lying around. It was like living in a fancy hotel.

Ever since her brother had left, she had noticed a

change in Trenton. She didn't know if John had said anything to Trenton or not, but what he had said to her was engraved on her mind.

"You can have your fancy man if you want, but he had better be good to you or he'll have to answer to the Holmes brothers and that's a fact."

She hugged that thought to her chest. If only Trenton saw her as something other than his daughter's tutor. Oh well, she sighed, sitting the box on the bed. She'd just enjoy her life one day at a time and let the future work itself out. At least Trenton seemed to spend more time at home and more time with her and Kelsey instead of behind a closed door in his office. She wasn't sure what had caused the change, but she wasn't going to fight it. A huge grin slowly spread across her face as she sat the box on the bed and started to unbutton her blouse.

She was dressed in record time. She had never had on such soft clothes. The leather boots were the correct size and the outfit was snug like they had been tailored to fit her curves. She stood in front of the full-length mirror, admiring how she looked. It was so amazing that she could put on a few expensive clothes and suddenly feel like she had gone from a caterpillar to a beautiful butterfly. She turned both ways, staring at herself from the side and from the back.

"Hummm. I don't know if I like that," she muttered. "That's the view he'll see." She stood examining herself and suddenly laughed out loud. She certainly wouldn't feel frumpy standing next to Jennifer, now. Yes, she felt beautiful and confident. "Life. Bring it on," she challenged her reflection. "I can take whatever you send my way." She stood a little taller as she turned and left the room to join the others.

"Daddy, who is driving up our road?" They had been riding for an hour and were almost back to the stable.

Trenton turned in the saddle, frowning as he saw Jennifer's car pull through the trees. Why was she here? It was a day off. He felt that she was stretching her job duties to an extreme, not to mention his patience. She had been hired as his social secretary, yet it seemed she wanted to organize and control his private life as well as his political life. She wasn't content to just arrange which social gatherings he would attend and which ones he would skip, she was now trying to wedge her way into his private life as more than an employee.

He had noticed on several occasions that she acted like a jealous girlfriend, placing her hand on his arm or steering him away from conversations with other women. The first day Jennifer arrived at work wearing the diamond and opal ring on her left hand, one of the other secretaries had even congratulated him on his engagement. No, Jennifer was too much like his wife. She was all fluff and no substance. All she thought about was parties and having fun, but could care less about politics, world hunger, or the Middle East crisis.

"That's Miss Jennifer," Kelsey said, like she was announcing the devil himself. Disgust was written all over her face.

"Kelsey," her father admonished.

"Yes, sir," she mumbled, hanging her head.

Natalie rode up beside her and patted her leg, smiling and winking as they neared the stable.

Kelsey lagged behind when they started for the house, causing Natalie to walk slower. When her father was out of range to hear, Kelsey turned to look up at her teacher.

"Do you like Miss Jennifer?"

Natalie wasn't sure how to answer the question.

"I think she can be nice," she hedged.

"But she isn't always nice. And she doesn't like me."

"Honey, I'm sure you're wrong about that. Everyone loves you. There's so much about you to like that I can't even count all the things," she smiled at the sulking child.

"No, she doesn't. I heard her tell Mr. Andrew that children shouldn't be heard."

"You mean 'children should be seen and not heard'?"

"Yeah, something like that. She doesn't want me around. She only wants my dad, but not me. She once said that kids were worse than dogs. The dogs you could give away, but not kids."

Natalie was shocked, not only that Jennifer had said such horrible things, but also that she would say them where a child could hear her. That was cruel.

"Well, we'll just try to stay out of the way when she comes over, okay?"

They watched as Trenton reached the car where she

was sitting, waiting for them to walk over from the stable. Even though they had slowed, they were only a few moments behind him.

"Well, what a lovely surprise," Jennifer said, stepping out of the car. "Out for a little ride? It must be nice, Natalie, to be able to enjoy all the benefits of being rich and not have to pay for anything."

Natalie glared at the woman for a couple seconds before excusing herself, ushering Kelsey up the steps and into the house.

"Jennifer, I don't think I have to tell you that you're walking on thin ice here. I'm getting sick and tired of you coming to my home and being rude to my employees."

"I'm sorry," she smiled, looking anything but sorry. "I didn't mean to be rude," she cudgeled, shrugging her shoulders and smiling innocently. When his expression didn't change, she continued. "Anyway, I just dropped by to tell you that I was by the office a little while ago and I found out that the computers are fixed. Tomorrow we'll be back in business."

"You drove all the way out here to tell me that when you could have called?"

"Well, that wasn't the only reason I came by," she said, looking up through her long lashes and tossing out a coy smile. "I was hoping you'd offer me a cool drink and we could sit out on the porch or maybe have lunch together. I miss how we used to meet for lunch occasionally. I miss our stimulating conversations." She took hold of his arm and smiled up at him as she guided him toward the house.

"Why don't you run along upstairs and change into something more comfortable than those tight riding britches, although I must say they make you look very dashing, sir." She smiled up into eyes that were dark and brooding. She hated it when she couldn't tell what he was thinking. "I'll ask the cook to get us a pitcher of something cold to drink, and we can go over the notes on the dinner you're hosting. It's right around the corner, you know. Okay?"

"All right," he sighed. Sometimes it was easier to go along than to fight with the woman. In an hour he'd run her along so he could get in to the office and get some work done. Anything was better than spending too much time with her.

Natalie was brushing out her hair when there was a light tap on the door just before it opened an inch and a small eye peered into the room.

"Can I come in?"

"Sure, sweetie. Here, hop up on the bed and I'll brush your hair."

"Is that woman still down there with my daddy?"

"I don't know. If you really want to know, run down the hall and go out on the balcony to see if her car is still here," Natalie suggested. She felt a little guilty for suggesting the child find the answer to the question that was uppermost on her own mind, but she would rather die than have Trenton come upstairs and find her checking to see if Jennifer's car was still there.

"Okay. Be right back," she smiled quickly before hopping down and tearing out of the room.

Within a minute she was back. "I can't hear what they're saying, but I think they're having a fight. They're out by her car and they're not touching," she reported, grinning. "Maybe she'll go home and never come back."

"Kelsey, please don't say that. You must be polite to all the guests who visit your home."

"But she's not a guest. She works for him." Her wisdom was beyond her years, but Natalie continued to give her a direct stare.

"Yes, ma'am," she mumbled. After a moment she looked up. "But do I have to like her?"

Natalie could no longer keep her smile from showing. "No, honey, you don't have to like her," she said, reaching over to gently pull her into her arms for a big hug.

"Can we trot some more?" Ever since Kelsey had learned to trot, she wasn't satisfied to simply walk the pony.

"You do as you're told, Miss. We can't run the poor animal all morning. He needs a bit of a rest," Clyde admonished her. "We'll take them down by the lake and let them drink and then they'll be ready for a trot on the way home."

"Yes, sir," she mumbled.

Natalie hid a smile as she watched the dark curls bob up and down as the pony made his way down the slope toward the water. She knew Kelsey loved the pony and would never want to hurt it. She just had to learn to put the needs of others, people and animals, ahead of her own fun. She was young so there was time to learn the difficult lesson, but she was glad to see that Clyde was attempting to start the training at an early age.

She was surprised when her cell phone rang. It was so peaceful in the trees near the lake that the shrill ring was out of place.

"Hello?"

"Miss Natalie, this is Carmen, the cook's helper?"

"Yes, what's wrong?"

"Well, the cook slipped on the floor and fell. I think her leg is broken and I can't find Andrew anywhere. What should I do?"

"Have you dialed 911?"

"Yes, ma'am. They're on the way." Her voice was shaking, but she was able to get the words out.

"Good. Keep her quiet and cover her with a light blanket. We'll be there in a few minutes. Just stay calm." When she flicked the phone shut, she turned in the saddle to look back at Clyde.

"Clyde, do you have any idea where Andrew might be?"

"Yes, ma'am. He was going into town this morning to a doctor appointment."

"Darn," she said under her breath. After a moment, she made a quick decision.

"Listen, they need you back at the house right away. The cook has fallen and probably broken her leg and the assistant is scared silly. You can get back faster by yourself, so go ahead and Kelsey and I will turn around and follow you."

"I'm not supposed to allow you two to ride out by yourselves," he countered.

"The pony can't go as fast and they need you back there just as fast as you can get there. We'll be fine for the twenty minutes it will take us to get home. Go on. If Trenton gets angry, I'll just explain the emergency and take all the flack. Okay?"

"I don't know. Mr. Lancaster said . . ."

"Don't worry about it. We'll be fine."

"Okay, but hurry. I don't want you out here alone any longer than absolutely necessary." As soon as the instructions were out of his mouth, he whirled the horse around and headed toward the house at a gallop.

Kelsey was wide-eyed as she watched him go. "Will Mary be okay?"

"Oh, I'm sure she'll be fine. She'll just have to go to the doctor, and they'll fix her right up," she assured the little girl. "In the meantime, let's turn around and head for home."

It took less than twenty-five minutes for them to get to the stable. When they topped the hill they saw the ambulance pulling away from the house. Andrew was standing beside his dusty blue pickup that had apparently been stopped in a hurry since it was sitting at an angle and the driver's door was still standing open.

She was glad to be able to turn the reins of their horses over to the stable boy and hurry over to the house to find out how Mary was doing.

As she approached, Andrew turned on her, fury blazing in his eyes as his lips thinned. Natalie hesitated for a moment, unsure what he was so angry about. She had never seen him this angry, but she couldn't imagine he was this upset with the cook for getting hurt. That didn't make any sense.

"How is she?" Kelsey had moved up to take her hand, squeezing it as she snuggled close to Natalie's leg. Without thinking, Natalie's other hand reached across to stroke the child's head.

"When you get Miss Kelsey taken care of, I'd like to speak with you alone," he told her.

She was concerned about how Andrew looked. His face was flushed and his hands had a slight tremor as he glared across the few feet that separated them.

Why had he been to the doctor? Was he sick? Or was the red face and trembling due to his obvious efforts to control his anger? She stood for a couple moments before moving.

"Come on, Kelsey, let's go up and take a quick shower and change our clothes, and then you can sit in the kitchen with Carmen and have your lunch while I talk with Mr. Andrew. Okay?" For once, Kelsey was quiet.

Her nodded head was the only answer, but her eyes followed Andrew as he turned on his heels and stomped toward the stables.

"Is he mad at us?" She was now staring at Natalie as she waited for an answer.

"Oh, I don't think so, honey. Why would he be angry with us? We didn't do anything." They turned and started toward the steps as the next question came.

"Well, is he mad at Mary?"

Natalie gently laughed as she started up the steps. "I'm sure he's not. It's not her fault that she slipped and fell. I can't think of any reason for him to be angry with her. Maybe he's just frowning because he's worried about her," she told the child, trying to convince herself as well as Kelsey that there was nothing to worry about.

It was a little past noon before Natalie could get away and head down to the stable. The sun was almost directly overhead, beating down mercilessly on her uncovered head and arms. She had changed into linen slacks and a matching blouse, but due to the high humidity she felt like she needed another shower.

It was a relief to step into the shaded coolness of the stable.

"Hey, Billy," she said, waving to the stable boy who was raking new straw into a stall.

He ducked his head and kept working, gradually turning to face another direction.

"Well," she muttered aloud. "That doesn't bode well

for this visit. Andrew must be in a real dither if he's been taking out his anger on his favorite stable boy."

She tapped lightly on the foreman's door, taking a deep breath and releasing it slowly while waiting for him to tell her she could enter. The office was small, the metal desk taking up most of the floor space, only leaving her room to stand.

"Hi, Andrew. You wanted to see me?"

Andrew looked up at her over the top of his half-glasses for several seconds before taking them off and leaning back in the chair.

"It's a good thing that it took you so long to get over here. It's given me a chance to cool off before I talk to you." He laid the glasses on the desk, never losing eye contact with her. He was no longer glaring at her, but she could tell that he was still upset.

Natalie felt the tightening start in her stomach and work to all her extremities. What was going on? What was he talking about? Why was he so angry with her?

"Do you even know what you did?"

Her mind was on a rampage to figure out what was wrong, but she was coming up empty. She didn't have a clue. She feared that she was somehow going to be held accountable for what happened to the cook, even though that didn't make any sense. She shrugged her shoulders as she shook her head.

"No, Andrew. I don't have any idea what's going on."

"Well, I want you to know that I really liked you

when I met you." He took a deep breath and released it in a huff. "I thought we could trust Kelsey with you."

She was growing weak with dread. Was he going to fire her? Did he have the authority to fire her?

"When you first started, Mr. Lancaster told you that you were never to take Kelsey out without having a guard with you, remember?"

"Well, of course I do," she answered, still frowning as she tried to understand. "I've always had you or Clyde with . . ." She stopped in mid-sentence as she realized where this must be headed.

"Is this about my sending Clyde back and riding in alone with Kelsey?" She couldn't believe this.

When he nodded, she took two steps forward until her legs bumped into the desk, her fists clinched at her sides as she leaned over the scattered papers, her eyes shooting arrows at the aging man.

"That's ridiculous. There was an emergency and he was needed back at the house." She was glad there was a desk between them. Otherwise, she might have been tempted to take a swing at the man, even though he was bigger and older. This was stupid and she was angry enough to bend steel using her bare hands.

"First of all, it wasn't life or death, only a broken bone, and"—he held up his hand for her to hold her comments until he had finished—"and what if it had been a ruse? What if someone had held a gun to Carmen's head and told her to call you? What if it had been a setup just to get Clyde away from you two since everyone knew Trenton and I were both gone?" His voice was low and under control.

Natalie stepped back, shaken to the core as she fumbled to brace herself and not have her legs buckle under her. Her arms were shaking as her mind wrapped around what he had just said. She hadn't given it a thought. She had just reacted to the call without thinking of possible danger to Kelsey. She had failed at her job. Her eyes refocused on Andrew when he spoke.

"I can see that you now understand why I was so angry when you got back. At least you got back safely, but that was luck."

"I'm sorry. I never thought about it being a lie."

"Even so, it was not reason enough to break protocol." He rubbed his darkly tanned hands down his face, closing his eyes for a moment before continuing. "Trenton is on his way home, and I've got to tell you that he's furious. Thankful, but furious."

"I understand." After a moment's hesitation, she took a deep breath and looked the older man straight in the eyes. "I want you to know that Clyde had nothing to do with the decision. In fact, when I told him to head back alone, he said that he shouldn't leave us alone. I told him I'd take credit for the choice, so I'd appreciate it if you'd not fire him or anything for my error in judgment."

"He'll answer for his own stupidity, but not with his job. He knows the rules and just because his . . . just because Mary was injured was no reason to break protocol."

She noticed the hesitation and change of words, but

didn't waste any time pondering what he had first planned to say. Right now her mind was too weighted down with what was happening or about to happen.

"I am so sorry that I got him in trouble," she said, her eyes dropping to focus on the papers in front of Andrew.

"Natalie, don't take credit for his stupid mistake. He's a grown man and knows he shouldn't have gone off and left you. It was his decision, his choice. So I don't want to hear another word on that, you hear me?"

She shrugged her shoulders in answer. After a moment she raised her eyes again. "You've known Trenton for years. Should I start packing?"

He sat looking at her for several seconds before answering. He saw apprehension and dread in her eyes, but he had to be truthful. He wouldn't lie to her.

"I honestly don't know. It could go either way. Since losing his wife, Kelsey has been his first priority and this is the first time there has been a breach of security since she arrived here, so I just don't know." He didn't smile, but his eyes softened when he added. "I know he likes you a lot and thinks you're wonderful for Kelsey, so who knows?"

She nodded. There wasn't anything else to say. Whatever would happen would happen and there was nothing she could do to change things now. She'd just have to wait for Trenton to get home. She couldn't stop the shudder that shot through her body. For the first time since she had taken the job, she dreaded Trenton getting home.

"I'll be in my room." She gripped the edge of the desk

for a moment to steady herself before turning. Almost to the door, she stopped to look over her shoulder. "Thank you."

Her words came out so softly that he had trouble hearing them. He could hear the quiver in her voice, but he admired her guts. She had been ready to fight, but when faced with having broken the rules, she hadn't tried to squirm out of responsibility. In fact she had tried to take all the blame. He admired her and hoped Trenton wouldn't fire her. They all needed her.

Her daddy was angry. She crept closer to his office door, cringing as she realized that he was yelling at Miss Natalie. Why was he so angry? Why was he blaming Miss Natalie for Miss Mary breaking her leg? Tears streamed down her face as she huddled by the door and listened.

"I can't believe you were so stupid that you'd go against what I said and go out riding alone," he said, standing on his side of the desk, his body leaning forward against his hands that were palm down on the glass.

"We weren't alone until . . ."

"I know what happened," he thundered. "You don't have to fill in any details." He stood and walked from behind the desk to pace back and forth.

"I thought you understood the danger. I thought they informed you all when you were put on the approved list. I thought I could trust you," he said, his voice lowering as he stopped and glared at her. "Maybe you don't understand the gravity of the situation." He stood for several moments, just staring at her before he sighed and motioned to the chair facing his desk. "Have a seat, and I'll explain," he told her. His voice had softened as the anger drained from his face.

He looked tired, like the weight of the world was balanced squarely on his shoulders. She moved quietly to one of the cushioned chairs he had indicated and perched on the edge, her hands clinched together in her lap.

"I'm heading up an investigation into genocide and other atrocities in several countries by known terrorist groups. I'm to report my findings to the United Nations in a couple weeks along with my recommendations about trade sanctions and embargos because the countries involved are harboring these terrorists.

"There have been several threats to my life and even to my family, but lately the threats have seemed more credible. In fact," he said, never losing contact with her eyes, "someone got into my office, hacked into my computer, and then disabled things for a couple days."

She had never felt so low in all her life. There were threats against his life, as well as Kelsey's, and she had added to his worries.

"The computers are back up and working, but we don't know how much information was seen. At least the files are all still intact, but there were lists of names, witnesses, that we didn't want to become public." He walked to the desk, leaning back against it almost in front of Natalie.

Natalie knew that he no longer trusted her and with good reason. Considering the danger to Kelsey from terrorists and people who didn't like Trenton because of the work he was doing for the United Nations, she knew he couldn't afford to take any chances. He was right. She didn't have a defense. She had known better, but under the stress of the moment she had made a wrong decision.

"What I'm saying is that there are always threats, but lately the credibility of the threats has intensified. I won't take a chance with losing my daughter."

"All I can say is that I'm sorry and even though nothing happened to us, that's no excuse considering what could have taken place." She had to force herself to keep eye contact with him. And to think she had fantasized being married to this man. Well, no chance of that. He'd marry her when hell froze over.

"I don't know what else to say to you. I'm at a loss for words," he heaved another sigh.

"I can be packed and out tonight as long as Andrew or Clyde can give me a ride into town to catch a bus," she said, standing.

The words were barely out when the door flew open and a tiny body shot into the room.

"No! No, I won't let you go. I won't!" She stomped her foot as her small arms wrapped around Natalie's legs, her face buried against the slacks that were now absorbing the child's tears.

"Oh, honey, don't cry," she pleaded with the sobbing girl as she stooped to gather her in her arms. "Shhh, it's going to be all right." She lifted sorrowful eyes to Trenton who had stood up when the door had banged against the bookcase.

He looked helpless as he watched his daughter in the arms of the woman that he was growing to care about, the same one who had put his daughter in danger because of a poor decision. He released a breath he had been holding, closing his eyes to give himself a few moments to decide what to do.

Trenton reached down, taking Kelsey by the shoulders to pull her away from Natalie.

"No!" Her shriek reverberated off the walls as she kicked and cried, striking out at her father as he gathered her in his arms and held her tightly against his chest while she fought. When she had used up her energy, he relaxed his arms enough to allow him to lean back and look into eyes flooded in tears.

"Were you listening to our conversation?"

"It wasn't a conversation. You were yelling," she accused. Her eyes narrowed, glaring with accusation at her father, her bottom lip sticking out when she puckered her mouth in anger.

"It was still a private, grown-up conversation that you had no business listening to. If we wanted you to hear us talking, we would have done it at the dinner table."

"You don't allow yelling at the table," she reminded him, her tone bordering on rudeness.

"Well, I want you to go back upstairs and one of us will come to get you when it's time for dinner. You're to play in your room until then, okay?" He was still holding her, but she was stiff as a board. Her jaws were locked and determination shot from her eyes like arrows. He was going to have his hands full when she got older. She could be just like her mother at times.

"Go on," he stepped back and urged her toward the door with a gentle push on her back. It was breaking his heart to see her so upset, but he was dealing with the situation the only way he knew how. It hadn't passed his notice that she hadn't been this upset since she had lost her mother. Was she so attached to Natalie that she would feel the loss like losing her mother all over again? Lord help him, how should he handle this?

Natalie stood watching the child, her own heart breaking as the child cried. Never in a million years would she have thought she would be so affected by a child's tears. Kelsey had cried like her little heart was broken and it was all her fault. If only she had made the right choice. If only she had thought. If only . . .

Kelsey turned enormous glistening eyes toward Natalie, taking a step closer as Natalie stooped down and reached out to take the child's hands.

"Promise me you'll be here tonight to read me a story and tuck me in?"

Natalie knew she was begging to know that things wouldn't change if she left the room. She didn't know how to fight the emotions that were weighing everyone down, but she could ask for a promise that at least that evening things would be the same. She couldn't promise about tomorrow since that was in Trenton's hands, but she could give the child this one promise.

She glanced toward Trenton, searching his dark stare for any indication on whether or not she could make the promise. When he didn't say anything, she took a breath and took a risk.

"Yes, honey. I'll be here tonight when you go to bed and, yes, I'll read you a story and tuck you in. Now, while you're waiting for one of us to come up and get you for dinner," she said, smiling as she wiped tears from the soft cheek, "why don't you read Marisa a story. And before you know it, I'll be there. I promise," she said, using one finger to make a cross over her heart.

Tiny arms flung around Natalie's neck for a quick tight hug before she ran from the room and stomped up the stairs. When the door to her bedroom slammed, both adults released their held breaths.

Natalie didn't know what to say. She stood waiting for the verdict. Would the ax fall, or would she be given a second chance?

"I have to think. We'll discuss this more in the morning. Go on up to Kelsey. She's waiting and she needs you right now," he concluded, turning his back on her and returning to sit at his desk.

She didn't have to be told twice. She paused only long enough to pull the door shut on her way out. Once in the hall, she leaned against the wall and willed her body to stop shaking. What would he decide? With her mother, sleeping on it meant that she would be less angry by morning and she would give a much more fair answer. However, with her grandfather, the extra time had only served to give him more time to stew. If anything, he would be angrier the next day. Which way would Trenton be?

"Well," she said out loud as she climbed the stairs. "This decision is out of my hands. If I'm fired, I'm fired. But if he gives me a second chance, I'll never make another snap decision that will impact Kelsey's safety." Cross her heart and hope to die.

Chapter Nine

"Trenton, I just heard and had to call you right away. Isn't it awful? I couldn't believe it when I was told how careless your nanny was today with poor little Kelsey. The child must be frightened half to death," Jennifer said, her shrill voice carrying over the phone wire to irritate him while he sat drinking brandy.

"Well, it wasn't as bad—"

"You don't have to make light of the situation on my account. I know you like the woman since she's been doing such a good job up until today, but you have to admit that there are a lot of good teachers, so you don't have to keep her just because she's smart. No, in fact, you can't afford to keep her in the house since she so blatantly put Kelsey's life in danger. You have a responsibility as a father to do whatever is necessary to keep your child safe."

He was having a hard time wrapping his mind around the fact that someone had told Jennifer about things happening at his home. Only a few hours had passed and she already knew. And now she was telling him who to hire and who to fire. Well, he had to admit, he had asked for her input on hiring a tutor, so maybe she thought she had a right to input on firing that person. But she was wrong.

"Jennifer, I don't think this is any of your business. I can handle it."

"Oh, Trenton, I know you can, but why should you have to? That's why you have employees in the first place. We can do the dirty work for you. Besides, I feel partially responsible since you hired her in the first place because of my recommendation. I mean, even though there was a mix-up with the names and the wrong one was called, it was still my fault that the wrong girl was called."

"Jennifer, you don't have to blame yourself. We're very happy with Natalie. We just have to work through this rough spot right now, that's all." He was tired and needed to rest. He had put in a long day at the office and then had come home to utter chaos, including a hysterical child. He needed this drink, he thought, staring at the brandy snifter. And some peace and quiet. He needed to think.

"I'll talk to you tomorrow at the office," he told her.

"But, you know—"

"Good-bye, Jennifer." He slammed the receiver into the cradle, wishing he could throw it across the room. It would give him a sense of release if he could throw something, or hit something, or . . . or maybe just hold Natalie in his arms. He had been unable to get the woman out of his mind ever since he had kissed her out on the balcony under the stars.

Every time he closed his eyes he could smell her perfume and feel her hand slide up into his hair. Every time he stepped inside the house, he was looking for her smile. Every night at the dinner table, he was wishing they were somewhere alone and every night when he climbed the stairs to go to bed, he wished he wouldn't have to sleep alone.

More than once he had awoken in the middle of the night, breathing heavy and sweating, only to realize that he was in bed alone. Once she had invaded his home, she had quickly invaded his thoughts and even his dreams.

"God, what am I going to do?" He sat in the high-backed leather chair and stared at the ceiling. Even as he sat thinking about her she was upstairs with his daughter, trying to give the child what she needed; trying to give the child a feeling of security in a world turned upside down. Could he find another Natalie? Someone who would love his daughter as much as she appeared to love Kelsey?

Jennifer was right about one thing, he thought. There were a lot of good teachers out there, but there weren't as many women who would care for Kelsey like Natalie did. A lot of women had children, but not all of them made good mothers.

He allowed his mind to wander back to his wife for a few moments before shaking himself. There was no use looking back to that time. There was nothing to be gained from pondering the what ifs.

"That's it. That's my answer," he said out loud. "There's nothing to be gained from worrying about what ifs concerning the lapse of security surrounding Kelsey. Everyone has learned a lesson, so we have to move on." With that decision made, he smiled as he slid back the chair and went to check on dinner. Suddenly he was starving.

When they all sat down to dinner that evening, everyone felt uncomfortable, but Trenton soon had his daughter laughing as he told stories about when he was a kid in England and how much trouble his trainer had teaching him to ride horses.

Natalie began to relax when he looked over at her and winked. She wouldn't be fired. He had come to terms with her transgression and was giving her a second chance. She vowed that he wouldn't be sorry for trusting her.

After dinner they worked on a puzzle set out on a card table in the den until time for Kelsey to get ready for bed. When they stood to leave the room, Trenton reached out and touched Natalie's arm.

"Can I speak with you for a moment?"

His eyes were kind. She knew she had nothing to worry about.

"Kelsey, honey, why don't you go up and slip on your nightgown and I'll be up in a minute to read you a story and tuck you in."

The child hesitated for a moment, looking between her father and Natalie.

"Daddy, are you coming up to say good night?"

"Yes, honey. I'll be up to hear your prayers and to kiss you good night," he assured her, brushing stray hairs back from her forehead. She reached over and hugged her father before she turned and ran out the door.

"I just wanted to tell you that you don't have to worry about your position here. I want you to stay." He reached across and touched her hand lightly as he continued. "You've been great for Kelsey. I've seen a huge change in her confidence and I want you to know I appreciate all you're doing. As to what happened today, I overreacted a little; however, please don't ever be alone without security in the future." He pulled his hand back before he gave in to the desire to pull her into his arms and kiss her until she begged for mercy.

"Um, thank you. I promise you won't be sorry." She stood, sending him a quick grateful smile before leaving the room.

"I'm not too sure about that," he spoke aloud after she was gone. "You have disrupted my thoughts, my dreams, and my work. I just might be very sorry I'm keeping you here," he muttered, walking around the table and heading for his office.

The following morning the doorbell rang while they were having breakfast.

"I'll get that, sir," the maid said, sitting the coffee carafe on the table near Natalie's elbow.

"I've come to pick up Mr. Lancaster," came the familiar voice. "Is he down yet?"

Trenton sighed deeply as he laid his napkin on the table and stood. Just as he turned, the phone rang.

"Hi, Jennifer. What brings you here this morning?"

"Excuse me. The call is for Miss Natalie. She said she's your mother," the maid said, holding the phone toward Natalie.

"Oh. Would you all please excuse me? I'll step into your office, if that's all right?" She glanced at Trenton, waiting for his answer.

"Certainly, take your time."

She left the dining room, her voice growing more distant as she got further away.

Jennifer stood, watching Natalie leave, holding her words until the other woman was out of sight.

"She's still here?"

"Yes, and that's enough on the subject," he told her, sliding his eyes over toward Kelsey.

"Yes, okay. It's just that I'm surprised. I don't understand," she said, sitting down at the table beside Trenton. The maid sat an empty coffee cup in front of her and poured coffee.

"Well, like I said," he emphasized, his eyes boring into hers, "it's settled. You don't have to understand any of my decisions."

She sat straighter, her eyes narrowing before relaxing and glancing away to reach for the cream. "Well, anyway, I thought I'd drop by and pick you up so we could talk about the party you're hosting this coming weekend. We can talk on the way in if you'd like since I know you'll be tied up the rest of the day in meetings. Is that all right with you?"

"Yes, that's fine. Give me a moment. I have to run upstairs and put on my tie and grab my jacket. It won't take more than a couple minutes. Just sit and enjoy your coffee."

Without a word, Kelsey slipped from her chair and left the room with her father.

Jennifer was furious. Her plan for getting rid of Natalie wasn't working. It appeared that the tutor had gotten to Trenton. He should have fired the woman and then it would have been easier to get him to send Kelsey off to a boarding school. If he had fired her, she might have been able to convince him that it was just too much trouble trying to keep a good nanny. Besides, she thought, the kid was in the way of her plans to get Trenton to marry her.

She stood, unable to sit still any longer. "There has to be a way to discredit that woman," she whispered. "There has got to be a way." All she had to do was figure out what it was.

She paced for just a moment before strolling through the living room toward the office. When she could hear Natalie's voice, she stopped to listen.

"Yes, mother," she laughed softly. "He is definitely feeding me. Honest, I'm fine." After a pause while Natalie listened to what was being said by the other person, she answered. "The house? Yes, it's beautiful. It's huge with lots of fancy decorations, and there are trees and a lake and even horses. Mom, you're not going to believe this," she laughed out loud, "but I'm learning to ride a horse."

There was silence while she listened. "Yes, honestly. I never thought I'd ride a horse, but actually it's fun." After a moment, "Yes, it was good to see him. He seemed to like Trenton, I mean, Mr. Lancaster and Kelsey." She was silent for a short time before she started talking again. "Yes, he seemed quite taken with Mr. Lancaster's collection of guns and knives. They both seem to enjoy hunting, although Mr. Lancaster said he hasn't done any since coming to America."

Jennifer had heard enough. What did she care about little Miss Natalie telling mommy about her new job and how lucky she was?

The idea slammed into her head like a bullet shot from a gun. Trenton's collection! She had read in Natalie's file that her brother had been in jail. Perfect. Without wasting a moment to ponder the outcome, only vowing to do anything to discredit Natalie in the eyes of the ambassador, Jennifer slipped through to the living room, lifted the glass top of the case, and pulled out one of Trenton's prize knives. Quickly tucking it under her jacket, she took the edge of her jacket to rub the fingerprints from the glass where she had put her finger and thumb, then lowered it back into place. She almost ran back to the dining room to slip the knife into her purse before Trenton came back downstairs.

Sitting down, she relaxed, crossing her legs gracefully to wait. Where there was smoke there was fire, and big brother's reputation should throw enough doubt toward Natalie for Trenton to get rid of her. She smiled as she lifted the coffee cup to her mouth to sip the rapidly cooling coffee.

It was the following afternoon when the maid was dusting the case and noticed the missing knife. She immediately informed Andrew, who had the employees check everything to see if anything else was missing. He hesitated calling Trenton at work until he gave them a chance to check the house. When nothing else appeared to be out of place, he put through the call.

"What? Are you sure?"

"Absolutely, sir. I had staff check the rest of the house to be sure nothing else is missing, but everything appears to be where it should be."

"Heaven forbid, but have you asked Kelsey if she was playing with any of my things?"

"Yes, sir. She was the first one I thought of, although it didn't seem to make sense that she would need one of your knives for her dolls," he cleared his throat. "Sir, I think we have to go under the assumption that someone in the house has helped themselves to one of your knives. I suggest calling the police right away to file a report."

"Yes, I guess we must do that. I'll try to get away soon and come home. Don't touch the case. I'm sure the police will want to dust it for prints."

"Yes, sir. I'll take care of it right away."

By the time he got home, the house had settled back into a sense of normalcy. The police had been there to take their report and dust for prints, but had been unable to get anything. He had already received a call from the chief of police and was satisfied that they would do everything they could.

He and Andrew had discussed the situation on the way home, but neither felt any of the employees in the house would have taken it. Only Natalie had been with him less than five years and most had worked for him more than ten years. They had each proven themselves to be very trustworthy.

When they pulled up in front of the house they continued to sit in the car, pondering their next move.

"Well, sir, we also have to look to outsiders who have been in the house since the last time Mattie dusted."

"Eliminating the police and the ambulance attendants since they were only in the kitchen and never alone, that leaves just Jennifer and Natalie's brother."

Each man stared at the other. The answer was obvious. The brother had been in prison. He had to be the one.

"Should we tell the police?"

"First, let me talk with Natalie. Would you call her for me? I'll be in the office." He hated the thought of confronting her with this issue so close on the heels of the breach of protocol with Kelsey, but he didn't have a choice.

He slid out of the car without waiting for Andrew to get out to open the door, making it into the house and ducking into the office before Kelsey knew he was home. He just wasn't up to her enthusiasm right now. All he wanted was peace and quiet and maybe a scotch.

His body felt heavy as he slumped into the leather chair, using his foot to swivel around to gaze out the window. He loved the view across the lawn and gardens, but today was one of those rare days when he hadn't looked forward to coming home.

He hoped he had a chance to talk with Natalie before Kelsey discovered he was home. He wanted to get this over with, not delay it until after dinner.

He dealt with confusion and controversy all day and wanted tranquility when he came home. It didn't look like tonight would be one of those nights. He hated having to accuse her brother. Every time he thought about Natalie and her brother, it was like comparing night and day. She was honest where he was deceitful. She was beauty and he was dirty and crude. But he had gathered enough from her personality to venture that if he attacked her brother, it would be attacking her family—in short, like attacking her.

He scrubbed his hand down his face before putting his fingers and thumb on each side of his head and squeezing his eyes between them. He was tired. He hated upsetting Natalie. He would rather have her in his arms and in his life forever, but she was too many years younger than him and it wasn't fair to ask her to take on a ready-made family, even if Natalie seemed to already love his daughter.

But his stomach tightened every time she walked into the room, even every time he heard her voice or smelled her perfume. He was addicted. She was like a drug that he felt he had to have. What was he going to do about her?

He just knew he had to take care of business first. As much as he hated losing the knife, he wasn't going to allow the incident to ruin his life. His anger surfaced again as he remembered the conversation he had with Jennifer before leaving the office.

"Oh I'm glad I caught you before you left for home. I couldn't believe it when your secretary told me about the theft at your home. I guess now you'll get rid of that tutor. She's not the one who should be around little Kelsey. She's a bad influence," she added, draping her body expertly in the chair facing his desk.

"Enough. Natalie had nothing to do with this." His voice had turned cold and stern.

"Are you sure?" When he continued to glare at her, she rushed on. "I couldn't help overhearing your secretary telling someone on the phone about the theft, so I did some research and found that one of her brothers was arrested and spent time in jail." She dusted imaginary lint from the front of her immaculate linen pants outfit.

"So, with that kind of background in her family, can you imagine how I felt? When I heard the report that one of your knives had been stolen I knew right away that it had to be her brother. Didn't you say he hunted? Interesting. You know, my first thought was that one of the servants had stolen it from you, but since her brother has a prison record, well, . . ." she shrugged her shoulders, shaking her head. "It's so sad about the little tutor."

Trenton knew Jennifer didn't feel sorry for Natalie, but he was definitely concerned about allowing any strangers into his home until he knew for sure who had taken the knife. He didn't care so much about his possessions, but his daughter was a whole other matter.

"You might as well just get rid of her. You can't trust her. Either moral issues were taught in the home or they weren't, and I'd bet honesty was a seldom-discussed issue when she was growing up."

"Jennifer, you can't blame her even if it was her brother who stole something. She didn't have anything to do with it."

"Really? How do you know? Didn't you say the only one stolen was also the most expensive one?"

"No, I didn't, and you seem to know a lot more about this than a social secretary should. Can you tell me what a burglary in my home has to do with what social event I'll be going to next or what food will be served at the party I'm giving next month?"

"Don't get upset with me, I'm just the messenger. Maybe you should ask her about her brother and his police record or maybe just fire her and put this mess behind you, but either way, you have to be concerned about having poor little Kelsey around such an influence."

The light knock on the door jerked him from his thoughts.

"Come in," he called out, swiveling back around, sitting up straighter in the chair.

"You wanted to see me?" She hesitated until he nodded and motioned for her to come in and sit down in the chair facing his desk.

"I'm not going to beat around the bush. I'm too tired to do anything except come straight to the point. As you know, someone has stolen one of the knives from my collection and the police have been notified. They've asked about people in the house other than staff and the only two, outside of police and ambulance attendants, are Jennifer and your brother."

He wasn't saying anything that she hadn't already ran through her mind. Her brother was the first person she thought about when the alarm was raised and the police called. She had even told the police about her brother visiting, but she had said that she didn't think it would be him since he had never stolen anything in his life that she was aware of. She had even volunteered that he had been in prison, but that was because he had lost his temper at a bar and beat up a guy. It hadn't mattered that the guy he had hit was guilty of swatting John's wife on the rear end; it had just mattered that he beat the man up, sending him to the hospital.

"I thought about my brother also, but he went to jail for three months once for beating up a guy who touched his wife inappropriately and that was almost eight years ago. I just don't think it was him," she said, shaking her head.

"Natalie, would you be willing to call him right now and put him on the speaker phone so the three of us can talk?"

"Sure. Anything to clear this up," she said, thankful that he was remaining calm.

After dialing her brother's phone number and pushing the button to put him on speaker, she sat back on the edge of her seat, waiting for him to answer.

"Hello?"

"Hi, Brenda. It's Natalie. Is Bubba there?"

"Hey girl! Yeah, hold on just a minute."

When he came on the phone, Natalie tensed. "Hi, it's me. I'm here with Trenton, and I have you on speaker phone," she told him.

"What? You calling to tell me you two are getting married or something?" His chuckle sounded low and tired.

"No." Her cheeks flushed, but Trenton took the lead, getting right to the point of the call.

"Listen, I asked Natalie to call so the three of us could discuss something that has come up here."

"Okay, what's up?"

"This morning the house cleaner noticed that one of the knives in my collection is missing from the glass case and the police have been here. There aren't any fingerprints, so we have no clue who might have taken it."

"So you're accusing me of stealing it?" His voice had dropped to a lower pitch and sounded hard.

"No, actually I'm not. I'm going to ask you once, for the record, but if you tell me that you didn't take it, I'm going to believe you."

"Why would you believe me?"

"First, because I have no reason not to believe you and secondly, because your sister has vouched for you. She said you have never stolen anything in your life."

"Well, she's right. My daddy made it clear to all of us that if we sinned, we'd go to hell and stealing is one of those sins. It's one of the Ten Commandments. She's right, I didn't take it."

"Okay, that's good enough for me. Since we had to tell the police the name of everyone who had been in the house, I wanted to warn you, just in case the police contact you."

"Okay, thanks. Was that all you called about?"

"Yes," they said in unison. Trenton smiled across the desk at her.

"Thanks, Bubba," Natalie said.

"Talk with you soon, Nat. Thanks, Trenton," he added before hanging up the phone.

"Do you believe him?" Natalie was holding her breath, waiting for his reaction.

"I'm not sure why, but yes, I do. Your brother is like a diamond in the rough. He's rough on the outside, but he seems to sincerely care about you. I saw him eyeing me, not the house or what was in it. It fit with his question as to whether or not we were announcing a wedding. I think he was sizing me up as a potential husband for his sister." He smiled, relaxing back into the chair. "In fact, I was . . ."

"Daddy!" The door flew open and a curly-headed whirlwind blew in. "I'm glad you're home. We had another exciting day. Today we had the police here. Who's coming tomorrow?" She scrunched up her face as if deep in thought as she climbed up into his lap to be hugged and kissed.

"You know, Munchkin, you should knock on a door when it's closed. Try to remember that, huh?" He stood, bringing her up with him as he kissed her again on the cheek. "Let's go see if dinner is ready. I missed lunch today and I could eat a horse."

"Daddy!" She looked horrified as she drew back to look into his face.

The deep rumbling laugh came up from his stomach. He threw his head back, laughing with true merriment.

Natalie sat for an extra moment before rising to follow them. It always left her feeling empty when she watched the two of them together. She wanted what they had. She wanted unconditional love. She had immediately fallen in love with the precocious child, but now she was pretty sure that she was falling in love with the father as well. She followed them with a heavy heart.

Chapter Ten

The warm summer days lulled Natalie into a pattern of work and play that left her craving a permanency that she never expected to have with Kelsey and Trenton. She was already thinking forward to the time when he would no longer be the ambassador and he and Kelsey would have to return to England. She never allowed her mind to linger on that line of thinking. She preferred to live each moment as it happened. The future would take care of itself.

She couldn't imagine life without the two people whom she had fallen in love with, so she chose not to think about it. Maybe she was being a coward, but it was just too painful.

Each morning she and Kelsey would take an hour to ride with either Andrew or Clyde, usually heading toward the lake or along the paths through the trees if the day was extremely hot. Kelsey was getting very good on her pony and was even talking about wanting a horse soon so she could learn to gallop.

So far Clyde had been able to talk her back down to the pony, telling her that he could teach her to gallop on Chester, but in order for her to ride a bigger horse, he would have to tie her in the saddle. She scrunched up her nose and didn't bring up the subject again, but Natalie knew it was only a matter of time.

The crisis was heating up again in the Middle East, and Trenton was spending longer hours than usual at the office.

"Will Daddy be home for dinner tonight?"

"I don't know, honey. I hope so, but I haven't heard yet."

"If he doesn't, can we sit out on the patio and eat?"

She felt sorry for the child. She missed her father, but even at her age, she already understood that her father had an important job and sometimes would have to spend more time away from home. The last few days had been long for Kelsey, hoping to see her father each evening and being disappointed.

"You know what? That sounds like a great idea," she smiled at the melancholy child. She had been asleep when her father got home the night before; unable to stay awake to get his hug and kiss. Natalie had wiped away her tears when she said her prayers and climbed into bed.

"In fact, even if he makes it home, why don't we ask him if we can. There's a nice breeze coming up from the lake and the patio will be in the shade. I think it would be nice and relaxing. Why don't we go ask Carmen to plan on it?"

"Okay." There was excitement in her voice again as she hopped off the sofa and ran toward the kitchen.

She had just disappeared into the kitchen when the front door opened and Trenton walked in. He looked tired, but she saw his eyes light up when he saw her.

"Hi. Hard day?"

"Yes. We'll be lucky if we can stall off an embargo crisis that could escalate into heaven knows what. I probably should have stayed at the office longer, but I just wanted to get home." He didn't add that he just needed to see her and Kelsey. In fact, he had thought about them off and on all day.

"Daddy!"

"Hi, Munchkin," he said, dropping his briefcase on the end of the sofa to gather her in his arms for a kiss.

"We're going to eat on the patio and we're having Mexican food and margaritas," she said. "Even me," she proudly announced. "Carmen says mine will be special."

"Special?"

"Um hum. She said it will be a virgin," she told him, her curls bouncing as she nodded her head.

Both adults chuckled as he placed her on her feet and reached up to loosen his tie before taking off his suit jacket.

Natalie never got tired of looking at his physique. He didn't seem to work out, well, except sometimes at the gym in the UN building, and yet he stayed in such toned condition. His face and neck were a golden brown next to the snow-white dress shirt, giving him a healthy, outdoorsy look that numbed her right down to her toes.

"Now that sounds like a plan," he told the child, skimming his large hand over her head and smiling down into her upturned face.

"Carmen said dinner will be ready in about twenty minutes, so if you get back quickly you'll have a few minutes to relax before it's served," Natalie said, her eyes raking over the man she was falling in love with. As she watched his gentle touch on his daughter's head, her body heated at the thought of those hands holding her. She had to drag her eyes away, breathing shallow and deep while she concentrated on controlling her thoughts that had run wild.

"Well, why don't I go upstairs and change into something more comfortable and then we can have those margaritas?" He had glanced up at Natalie when she abruptly turned and started walking toward the kitchen.

"We'll meet you out on the patio," Natalie said, tossing the comment over her shoulder as she quickly left the room.

He stood for an extra couple seconds, watching as the door between the living room and the kitchen swung back and forth on its hinges. What had set her off? She hadn't even waited for Kelsey to walk with her. Had he said something to upset her?

"Nah," he said in a low voice, "I must be imagining things." He jogged up the stairs and changed clothes in record time. It took him less than ten minutes before he strolled out to the table, tilting the umbrella slightly to keep them in the shade.

"Here, let me pour your drink, Daddy," Kelsey said, her tongue sticking out the side of her mouth as she concentrated on pouring the yellowish-green liquid without spilling it.

He lifted the salt-rimmed glass to sip the cool drink, closing his eyes to savor the unique flavor. "Um, very good. You did a great job mixing my drink, madam bartender," he teased her.

"Oh, Daddy, I didn't make it. You're silly," she giggled, flouncing over to her chair and plopping on the edge to lean forward and sip her drink.

There were so many things sticking out of her glass that he wondered how she could get the straw in to drink it. An umbrella listed to the side like a drunken sailor, and two spears with cherries and pineapple chunks bobbed in the liquid, with lime wedges balanced on the edge to complete the concoction. Well, it was nothing if not colorful.

"Dinner is served," Mattie announced, bringing a tray with three plates to the table. "Tacos and enchiladas with rice and beans. Hope you like it," she smiled.

"This looks fantastic. Thank you," Natalie added. She

didn't know how long Mary would be out with her broken leg, but Mattie and Carmen were doing a great job filling in. Maybe too good a job. There had been a lot more variety since Mattie had been cooking. They had more simple foods and everyone seemed to be enjoying it. Oh well, the cook situation wasn't her problem. That one was up to Trenton. She would just enjoy it while it lasted.

The sun was starting down by the time they finished, but it was still light. That was one of the nice things about summer. Even after the sun went down and the sweltering temperature started to abate, they still had time to enjoy the outdoors.

"Mr. Lancaster? Andrew is on the phone and he said it's urgent." Mattie was running as she held the phone out in front of her. Her eyes were wide with fright and her hand trembled as she passed over the phone.

"Yes?" He listened for only a moment before throwing down the phone.

"Kelsey, Natalie, follow me immediately and don't ask questions." He was already running for the back door. "Move!"

Her heart shot up to lodge in her throat, blocking off much-needed oxygen to her lungs as she leaped up, her chair flying backward as she shoved it. As she scrambled after Trenton, she grabbed Kelsey's arm to drag her along.

"What's going on?" Kelsey asked, stumbling as she was jerked over the threshold into the house.

Her eyes were huge, but there wasn't time to calm her. He knew their very lives might depend on how quickly they reacted. "Shhh," he ordered, grabbing her up in his arms as he raced through the kitchen, directing Natalie through the laundry room off the kitchen to a back staircase.

At the top of the stairs, he stood Kelsey back on her feet, grabbing her arm again as he ran for his room at the end of the hall.

Natalie's chest was aching as she sucked in air. She didn't know what was happening, but she knew to move when Trenton said to. It had to be a threat to their lives for him to scare Kelsey like this.

Kelsey was openly crying now, sobbing as she was propelled forward through the master suite and into her father's closet. Within seconds Trenton had shoved back a row of shirts, exposing a door in the wall. He punched in a code, and Natalie heard a click. He pulled open the door so hard that it slammed into the wall.

"Go! Down the stairs and then run and don't look back. I'll be right behind you," he ordered.

Natalie didn't wait to consider, but grabbed Kelsey's arm and jerked her through the opening, holding her up while they stumbled down the steps in the semi-dark. Kelsey was frantic now, her face contorted in a confused, terrified expression that broke Natalie's heart.

She heard the door close at the top of the stairs, cutting off what little light she had, but she didn't stop her descent. When she reached the bottom, she stumbled, righted herself, and pulled Kelsey forward, even as she heard Trenton bounding down the steps behind them.

Her breath was coming in short pants, her chest aching as she tried to continue without slowing down.

"Hurry," came the voice behind her. "We don't have much time. Andrew said several men climbed over the west wall and are headed toward the house."

She had so many questions, but not enough breath left to ask them. She had to conserve all her energy for putting one foot in front of the other. She was panting like she had run a marathon, but she knew it was fright that was slowing her down. She had to get her fear under control. Even though the threats had turned out to be real, the first priority was to get Kelsey out of harm's way.

Trenton picked up the child and took the lead, directing Natalie with one-word orders when the tunnel changed directions or dropped off. She didn't know how he knew when the tunnel was going to go right or left, but he always gave the direction change in time for her to adjust. It was like he had night vision.

She had no idea where they were headed, but she thought it was toward the stables. Why were they going there? Were they going to try to ride horses out of here? But they'd be in the open and it was too far to a town. They'd never make it alive. Why had he taken them out of the house? At least there were locked doors between them and whoever was out there if they were in the house.

She continued to run. She trusted his judgment. He

wouldn't take chances with their lives or his own. He had to figure, for whatever reason, that this was the best option. Thank goodness they apparently had an option, at least for now.

When they got to the end of the tunnel, he felt the wall until he found the keypad. After punching in the six-digit code, he shoved open the door and rushed forward into the office of the stable.

"Hurry." As she passed him, he slammed the door shut and pushed a button to lock the door. "This way and run!"

Once Trenton had picked up Kelsey, she remained quiet, latched around his neck with both arms, her face plastered to his neck as she jostled along in rhythm with his pounding steps.

"Get in the Jeep. In the back and hurry! Get on the floor and keep your heads down," he ordered, handing over the child.

Even as she was climbing in the back door of the vehicle, he was starting the engine, reaching for a garage door opener that controlled a door on the side of the stable.

When the door shut behind her, the Jeep shot out of the stable like an arrow from a bow. As he careened down a dirt road leading away from the backside of the barn, Natalie urged Kelsey into the well of the floor, hovering over her without putting her weight on the child.

"Who are they?" She managed to ask the question even though they were being bounced back and forth on the rutted road. She silently prayed that they would get out of this alive—and that she wouldn't throw up.

"I don't know. I've had intelligence reports saying there's been chatter that a terrorist cell wants to eliminate my family and myself. They don't want me voting next week. I've had extra guards watching the property and one of them spotted someone sneaking across . . ." He stopped speaking for a second when they heard rifles being shot.

"That's too close. Keep your heads down." He disregarded the Jeep and, pushing the gas pedal to the floor, he wrenched the wheel back and forth to keep it on the road. Between the ruts and the large potholes, they had a rough ride, but the Jeep held together and they were quickly in the protection of the trees.

They rocked around, bouncing once to land hard before the vehicle caught traction on the dry road and dug in to jerk forward again.

"Listen. Get up and sit near a door." She sat up, glancing at Trenton as he jerked the steering wheel back and forth trying to keep the Jeep in the middle of the road so it wouldn't hit any trees. "Natalie, when I slam on the brakes in a minute, I want you to jump out and pull Kelsey with you."

"No, Daddy! I don't want to leave you!" Kelsey screamed, starting to sob again.

"Do what I say! Natalie, run deep into the woods and hide there until I come for you. Do not show yourself to anyone but me, do you understand?"

"Okay. What about Andrew?"

"No one. Trust no one." The jeep rocked along for another few seconds before he called back to her. "Ready?" Without waiting for an answer, he slammed on the brakes, throwing them into the back of the front seats. "Now!"

Natalie jerked up the handle and stumbled out of the vehicle that hadn't come to a complete stop. Hesitating only a second to get her balance, she got Kelsey out of the way of the door and slammed it, turning into the woods without looking back.

She heard the Jeep leaving them, could even smell the dust in the air that the tires had kicked up as she ran through the brush, pushing limbs out of her way while she dragged Kelsey behind her. She had no way of knowing how far they had gone, but after several minutes she noticed a huge evergreen tree off to her right with limbs that hung over, touching the ground. She slowed to a stop and listened. When she was unable to detect any indication that they were being followed, she crouched down to look Kelsey in the eyes. Wiping hair from her face, she smiled reassuringly at the traumatized child.

"Are you alright, Sweetie?"

Kelsey was beyond talking. Her eyes were huge and blank, her breathing coming in short pants between sobs.

"Listen honey, we're going to find a place to sit down and rest and wait for your daddy to come back for us. Do you understand?" She waited until Kelsey nodded, then hugged her and stood, still holding her hand, to walk toward the tree. She could see space between the large bottom limbs where they could pass between and have room to sit and lean against the tree.

"Come on, through here. It'll be a little warmer, and we can sit and rest."

She was grateful that she could finally sit down. She had used up all her energy and any reserve created by the adrenalin rush of the flight. Once she had stopped running, it was as if the blood had drained from her body and her muscles had turned to mush.

She pushed pine needles into a large pile before sitting down and leaning back against the tree trunk. She pulled Kelsey into her lap, then leaned her head back and allowed her eyes to close. Her mind wanted to shut down and hide, but she had to stay alert.

What was going on? Was someone trying to kill Trenton? Or maybe kidnap Kelsey? Her body was shivering, but not from cold. Sweat was running down the side of her face and down across her ribs under her arms.

Her body began to shake violently as thoughts of Trenton being killed were allowed to creep into her mind. No! When her teeth started to chatter, her thoughts were drawn to Kelsey. The child was clinging and had started whimpering. Her thumb was in her mouth and her eyes were slammed shut to keep out the scary stuff happening all around her. Natalie hugged her tighter.

"Shhh, it'll be all right," she whispered. Her arms pulled Kelsey in a little closer as she began to rock, comforting the child as well as herself.

The sun had completely gone down now, and the day's

light was fading quickly. Tucked back inside the tree's limbs, she felt like they were wrapped in a cocoon, safe from the outside world, but she knew that could change in a moment.

Trenton fought to keep the Jeep on the dirt road that ran through the woods. It was not usually used for vehicles, only horses and possibly four-wheelers.

He could only pray that Natalie and Kelsey had gone far into the woods and that no one had noticed him stop the Jeep. He wasn't even sure anyone was chasing him, but he couldn't take a chance. He wasn't about to stop and find out. If someone were coming after them, then they'd know that the two girls weren't with him and would start scouring the woods. No, he couldn't take a chance.

Andrew's message had been, "they're coming across from the west." That's all he needed to hear to know to head through the tunnel to the stable. He was now headed in a eastwardly direction, making good time considering the poor condition of the dirt road, but wondering who might be waiting for him when he reached the paved county road in another half mile or so.

"God, I don't know if this is terrorists or what, but please take care of Natalie and Kelsey. Thank you," he breathed out just as he hit a pothole that bounced his head against the roof.

Before he realized what was happening, he cleared the woods and jetted out into the county road, slamming on his brakes as he jerked the wheel to the right. The vehicle started to turn before sliding across the road into the ditch on the other side where it came to a jolting stop.

He barely took time to release the breath that he had been holding before he stomped on the gas, kicking up dirt and gravel as the tires dug into the dry earth. He shot from the ditch onto the road like a slingshot, fishtailing for a moment until the tires gained traction.

He had gone less than a mile when he passed police cars racing toward his home, lights flashing and sirens blaring. Yeah, he thought, the cavalry has arrived. He continued, soon noting that he could hear a helicopter. It passed overhead before he could see if it was the police, a news channel, or unmarked which could be either the good guys or the bad guys. Only time would answer that question.

He stayed on the road for another mile, but when he didn't see anyone following him, he pulled into a gas station and drove around to the back. Once he was out of sight of the road, he parked and got out, quickly moving to the edge of the building so he could watch the traffic that passed without being observed.

Within two minutes he saw a blue pickup truck whiz by. He recognized the truck. It belonged to Clyde. Where was he going? He should be back defending the house and the employees. This didn't make sense.

Trenton and Andrew had set up a meeting place away from the house that they would take Kelsey to if there were ever a threat. He had confided in Clyde a few months ago since he was also responsible for the security and safety of the child. Now he was wondering if that had been a bad decision.

He wasn't even sure why he had dumped Natalie and Kelsey in the woods. That wasn't part of any prior plan. It had just hit him and in an instant he had made the decision to get them out of the vehicle and be the decoy, if necessary, to get the people away from the property. He continued to watch, waiting for Andrew to call him on the cell phone that was remaining ominously silent.

Mattie had nearly fainted when four armed men slammed through the front door, two of them running up the stairs to check the bedrooms and two rushing through the main level, their guns leveled and ready to use. When they had reached the kitchen, they had held her at gunpoint until the two came down the back stairs. The one who appeared to be the leader, although they all looked alike with their black outfits, ski masks, and gloves, pulled a cell phone from his pocket.

"No one here except a couple cooks. They're gone." He listened for a moment before motioning to the others with the barrel of his gun. They left through the front door, turning toward the stables.

Mattie sank into a chair for a moment, her legs too weak to hold her up. How had they missed finding them upstairs? She had seen them run up the back stairs. Did they hide in the attic and the men didn't look there?

When the shaking gradually started to lessen, she remembered what she needed to do. She rushed for the phone to dial 911.

"Westchester County Dispatch, what is your emergency?"

Before Mattie could even answer, she flinched as two shots were fired outside. They sounded to be a short distance away, maybe near the stable.

"Some men just broke into the house with guns, but they've left. But I just heard two shots fired outside."

"Is anyone hurt?"

"How should I know? I'm not going out there to look," she retorted indignantly.

"I'll send out a policeman to check it out."

"Thank you." When she hung up the phone she again sank into the chair. She couldn't believe she had been so rude to the woman on the phone. Her hands shook as she picked up her coffee mug to take a drink.

After a few minutes her mind returned to Mr. Lancaster. She hesitated only a moment longer before heading up the stairs, calling out for Kelsey and Natalie in each room before checking in the attic. It was like they had vanished into thin air.

Andrew had been on the east perimeter of the property when he got the call from their scout on the west. He scrambled to get to the four-wheel drive SUV he had used. He had been trying to reach Clyde at the barn but there was no answer, and he didn't want to call Trenton and chance giving his location away. Even though they had agreed to put their phones on vibrate in the event of an emergency, he wasn't ready to take a chance that Trenton had remembered. After all, he would have Kelsey and Natalie with him and he might have forgotten.

Andrew's vehicle slid to a halt in front of the stables. He didn't see anyone around, but he pulled a gun out from under the seat and ran to the side of the building where he cautiously made his way to the side door that stood open. A quick glance inside showed that the Jeep was gone. Thank goodness. That meant Trenton had been able to get the girls out. He darted back to the SUV, wasting no time getting up to the house to check and be sure everyone was all right.

The front door was standing open. As he reached the top of the stairs, he called out. "Clyde! Mattie!"

"I'm in here!"

When he entered the kitchen, Mattie was just coming out of the laundry room with a small fireplace shovel in her now relaxing arms.

"Clobber me with the shovel, would you?" He smiled for the first time since he had gotten the call.

"I didn't know if it was those men with the guns. Andrew, I can't find Mr. Lancaster, Natalie, or the little one. They're nowhere in the house. They've vanished," she said shrugging her shoulders.

"Don't worry about them. They're fine."

"How can you be sure?"

"I'm sure. Trenton wouldn't let anything happen to his little girl."

Trenton was not a patient man when it came to sitting around and waiting. It wasn't long before he left his post behind the building and got back into the Jeep. He wasn't doing any good hiding out here, looking for someone to drive by when he didn't even know who was following him. Staying here didn't make any sense at all.

With that decision made, he quickly got into the Jeep and headed toward the rendezvous spot. He had gone only a couple miles when he rounded a corner and slammed head-on into a blue pickup truck.

Chapter Eleven

Andrew finally gave in and pushed the button to dial Trenton. It rang four times before someone answered. The problem was that the person on the other end wasn't Trenton.

"Hello?"

"Clyde? Is that you?"

"Yeah," he said, his voice shaking.

"Where's Trenton?"

"Andrew, he's been in a wreck and he's out cold. I called the ambulance and I can hear them coming. I'll ride in with him," he offered.

"Was anyone else hurt besides Trenton?"

"He was in the Jeep by himself, and I don't know how bad he's hurt, but his head is bleeding and he's white as a sheet."

Andrew could hear the ambulance arriving. The girls weren't with him? That didn't make sense.

"Clyde, listen. Stay with him in the hospital. I'm going to make a call to get police protection on him in his room, but don't leave him alone. Do you have your weapon?"

"Yeah. I'm packing."

"Good."

"Do you know where Kelsey and Natalie are?"

"Clyde, I haven't got a clue. Take care of our man," he instructed.

When he hung up the phone, he was puzzled. None of this was making any sense. He knew the Feds were out looking for the men who had trespassed and threatened the ambassador, but the rest had him baffled.

Andrew paced back and forth while Mattie's eyes followed him. It was beginning to get on his nerves. He hated it when women hovered over him.

"Can I get you anything?"

"No," he said, turning to leave the room.

Outside, he stood on the porch, pondering what Trenton might have done. What would he have been thinking, and what would he have done to try to protect his daughter and the woman that he felt sure Trenton was falling in love with? He would have done almost anything to keep them safe. Even doing something that wouldn't seem to make much sense.

He stepped off the porch and strode toward the stable.

* * *

The sun had been down quite a while and the air was cooling off quickly. Natalie's rear end was numb, tingling every time she flexed her muscles or tried to shift a little.

Kelsey had fallen into an exhausted sleep, but her thumb was still stuck in her mouth. Natalie hugged her closer, shifting a little to the right at the same time.

Thank goodness they had just eaten or they'd be having a much more miserable time. She could sure go for some nice cold water, though. She prayed Trenton was all right and that he would be back for them soon.

As time passed, her mind wandered, thinking about what ifs that she hoped would never happen, yet wondering what she would do. Like, what if Trenton never came back to get them? How long would she stay hidden before they had to take a chance on coming out? Of course, she thought, the police would probably have dogs out looking for them before long, so maybe it was a moot point.

If she could keep her mind working she wouldn't go to sleep, and something told her that she shouldn't let her guard down. She was the only thing between Kelsey and danger and she'd die before she allowed the child to be hurt.

"Trenton, where are you?" Her whisper sounded loud in the darkness.

Her head jerked up and her eyes popped open when she heard a sound in the distance. Was it Trenton? She was tense, but she stayed utterly still as she listened intently.

Minutes seemed like hours as she waited, hearing someone calling, but not being able to make out what was being said. It was still in the distance, but it was coming closer. It sounded like someone was calling her and Kelsey, but it wasn't Trenton's voice.

When Kelsey roused and stretched, she gently took the child's face between her hands and put her mouth right at her ear.

"Kelsey, your daddy said not to come out of hiding for anyone except him. Do you understand?" When the little girl nodded her head, Natalie relaxed a little.

"Even if it's Clyde or Andrew, we are not to answer. Do you understand?" Again the child nodded her head.

"Kelsey, just hold on to me and don't be afraid. We'll be fine," she whispered. She pulled her closer, tucking Kelsey's head under her chin.

She didn't know about Kelsey, but she felt like crying.

Trenton came to in the emergency room. His eyes opened slowly, slamming shut when the bright overhead lights pierced through to his brain.

"Ah, Mr. Lancaster, you're awake. Good." A person was standing near his arm. "I'm Dr. Wilkins, and you're in the hospital. You had a pretty nasty crash, but everything seems to be in fairly good condition except your head, which took quite a hit."

"How long have I been here?" He was groggy, but he

had remembered the wreck and why he had been driving so fast.

"Oh, about ten to fifteen minutes, but . . . whoa, you can't get up," Dr. Wilkins ordered, pushing down on his chest to lower him back to the bed. "You have had a concussion and will have to stay laying down for awhile."

"I can't," he said, grimacing as pain shot through his temples. "You don't understand," he told the doctor, relaxing his muscles and closing his eyes.

"What don't I understand?"

"I'm an ambassador to the United Nations and someone is after me and my daughter is in danger. It wasn't an accident," he answered, his voice barely above a whisper.

"Don't move. I'll be right back." The doctor stepped out of the examining room and headed straight for the Nurses Station.

"Nancy, we need to immediately get Examination Room Three's name off the chalkboard and off the paperwork. He needs to be anonymous. Now he's William Anderson, got it?"

She looked a little confused, but nodded her head. "Yes, sir. Right away."

"Hurry. It's possibly life and death. And if anyone asks for him, he wasn't brought in. He doesn't exist as far as you know. Got it?"

"Yes, sir." The nurse picked up a chart and pulled some papers from it, replacing them with blank forms and handed the file to the doctor. As soon as he had it, he stepped over to the chalkboard and erased *T. Lancaster* and wrote in *W. Anderson*. Then he scribbled some notes in the folder before handing it back to the nurse.

"I need you to go over to the coffee room and the supply room and find the ambulance personnel who brought him in. If they're still there, tell them exactly what I just told you. Have them mock up phony paperwork and give you a copy for this file and remind them that they brought in W. Anderson. Got it? We'll get it straightened out later."

"Yes, sir. Can I ask why?" The middle-aged nurse had been requested to do many different things over the years, but this was unique. This was some kind of cover-up and she was curious.

"He's an ambassador from another country and he just told me that the accident he was in wasn't an accident. This is a life or death deal. James Bond-movie stuff," he smiled and winked at the woman who blushed to the roots of her bleached-blond hair.

"Okay, you can count on me. Just give me a second to get Alice to cover the desk here."

The doctor came around to the desk and picked up the phone. He punched the button for security. "Harold, this is Dr. Wilkins. I need a security guard down here, but I need the person to be dressed in scrubs and I'll explain the weird request later. Time is of the essence, so I've got to go. Can you do this?" After a moment, he nodded his head. "Good."

"Now," he said under his breath, "who do you call

when you have a dignitary you want protected and slipped out of the hospital? FBI, CIA, local police? Superman, yeah, that's who I'll call," he muttered.

He grabbed the phone book and flipped to the government pages. He didn't want this request to go through dispatch just in case someone was monitoring the channel. He had to smile as he thought about playing cops and robbers as a kid. The only problem was that if the guy was right, this was for real. If someone wanted the ambassador dead, as his doctor he had to do everything he could think of to protect the man.

It didn't take long for an orderly to report to Dr. Wilkins and ask which patient he was supposed to guard, and within thirty minutes a government official showed up asking to speak to the doctor.

"Mr. Lancaster?" When Trenton opened his eyes, using his hand to shield against the glare of the lights, he continued. "I'm Special Agent in Charge Doug Miller. I've been assigned to take you out of here and get you over to Langley where we can take care of you until you're well enough to go home."

"No. You're going to take me to my home so I can find my daughter and her tutor."

He spoke just above a whisper, but with such authority that the agent knew he meant every word. "Sir, I have my orders, and . . ."

"Agent, I don't give a damn about your orders. I have a child in danger and that trumps your orders. Now you either help me find her or you'll have to drug me to get me out of here to go to Langley. Do you understand what I'm telling you?"

"Yes sir. I need to make a call, but if you're sure then it's your choice."

"Thank you," he said, relaxing again when his head began to throb.

It took over an hour to get everything covered, but soon the agent was driving Trenton back toward the house.

"So, sir, can you tell me what's going on and why you think your daughter is in danger?"

"We've been hearing chatter that there are some factions who are unhappy with the way I've been voting on embargos. We heard that they were planning to take me out, so I had some extra men patrolling my place. When I got a call earlier, I was able to get my child and her tutor out of the house and deposited somewhere safe before I was in the accident. Now I need to get home to see how everyone is and get to my daughter."

"Have the authorities been notified?"

"Yes. I think that has all been handled, but I want to be sure before I bring my daughter back home. He could only imagine how frightened Kelsey and Natalie were, but if she followed his instructions, he felt sure they were alive and safe. But he had to know for sure.

When they reached his home, it was ablaze with lights. Every security light on the property was lit and almost every light in the house was on. From a distance it glowed like a beacon on the hillside. Even though his head still hurt and he was nauseated, he was glad to be coming home. He leaned forward, straining at the seat-belt to be home faster.

Agent Miller had been in touch with his superiors and the way was cleared for the ambassador to be taken home. Around the clock protection would be provided until those responsible for the breach of his property were found. According to the report, they had leads that they were following up on.

Trenton appreciated all they were doing, but all he really cared about was getting home and getting Natalie and Kelsey out of the woods. He felt sure he wouldn't find them at the house. He was positive they would still be out in the cold darkness.

When they rolled to a stop in front of the house, Mattie ran down the steps to open the door for Trenton.

"Oh, Mr. Lancaster, we've been so worried about you. We heard you had left with Miss Kelsey and Miss Natalie, and then we heard that you had crashed the Jeep. We've all been worried sick," she babbled on, taking his arm to help him up the steps.

Even before he took the first step Andrew came down to meet him, lifting one of Trenton's arms around his neck and allowing Trenton to lean on him.

"Trenton, we can't find the girls. We've looked all over, even the rendezvous point. Then I went into the woods calling them, but they aren't around. I'm afraid that they've been taken, sir." His eyes were hollow with fear and his normally ruddy complexion was pale with concern.

"Don't worry, Andrew. I know where they are. They should be fine. Cold and maybe a little frightened, but okay. I just need to get a policeman to go with me, and I think I'll be able to find them."

"Clyde's back from the hospital. He barely had any scratches."

"What are you talking about?"

"Sir, didn't you know? He was the truck you ran into on that curve. They took him to the hospital also, but he only had a few bruises. They released him almost right away and he came home and went out into the woods looking for Miss Kelsey and Miss Natalie. Bless him; he was so worried about them. He was truly distraught when he came back without them. He said he had been so sure he knew where they might be after he found out that they weren't in the Jeep with you when it crashed."

"Was anyone else hurt?"

"No sir, just scared. You said you know where they might be?" When Trenton nodded, he continued. "Let me help you back down the stairs and we'll go find them. The poor little tike must be scared half to death by now, not to mention cold."

"No, Andrew, I need you here to keep an eye on things. Especially the employees," he said, glaring into the eyes of his oldest, most trusted friend.

Andrew was silent for only a moment before nodding his head. "Very well, sir."

"Just help me down the stairs," he instructed.

"Miss Natalie," she whispered, "I'm cold." They had been sitting in total darkness for quite some time. Kelsey had dozed several times, but between those times, Natalie had been whispering as she told the child stories about when she was younger and living on The Hill back in West Virginia. Kelsey had forgotten and laughed out loud when she heard about the boys leaving her out in the woods overnight on a dare and how they had gotten in trouble when their mother found out.

"Here, sit between my legs and lean back against me. That will keep your backside warm." She already knew that the breeze was coming from behind them, so she would be the one getting the brunt of the chilly wind. She had long lost feeling in her rear end, accepting that it must still be there, even though she couldn't feel it to be sure.

She tried flexing her muscles to try to stimulate blood flow and revive them, but so far, no success.

"Miss Natalie, do you know what I wish?"

"What sweetie?"

"I wish you loved my daddy and I wish my daddy loved you so you could get married. Then I'd have you for my real-life mummy." She ran her hands down Natalie's arms until she reached her hand. The little girl pulled them toward her, kissing the back of one of her hands. "I love you, Miss Natalie. I wish you were my mummy, not just my tutor."

Natalie's eyes filled with tears. "Oh, honey, that's so sweet. I love you too." She sucked in a breath and held it for a couple moments trying to stem the tears that wanted to overflow while she laid her cheek on the top of Kelsey's head.

"If you married my daddy, would you have a baby?"

"Well, most people who get married have babies," she hedged.

"Then I'd have a little baby brother or sister," she whispered on a sigh. "That would be so neat. That would be better than having a horse or even a puppy."

Yes, Natalie thought, *that would certainly be neat.* It was already something that had crossed her mind several times, but she knew it would never happen. After all, Trenton didn't love her.

She intended to marry only once in her life and there was no way she would settle for just any man. She had her life mate picked out, but if he didn't want her, she'd just as soon stay single. Second best wasn't an option in her mind.

A shiver ran through her body as the breeze picked up, blowing the limbs around to brush against her arms. She fought her tendency to imagine animals or men just outside the edge of the limbs. Every sound made her flinch, but so far there had only been that one time when she had heard someone calling their names, but the person had never gotten very close.

She couldn't believe how brave Kelsey had been. She was so proud of the child. She couldn't have asked her to be any better than she had been, even when the man was calling their names and Kelsey had whispered that she had peed her pants a little. She hadn't whined or made a fuss, just informed Natalie and rushed to pee as soon as the voice started getting further away.

Natalie's thoughts were never very far from Trenton. She prayed again that he was safe and unharmed. It had been so long that she was beginning to be really worried. When she thought about him, invariably her thoughts wound back around to how she felt about him. Did she really love him? Oh yes. There was no doubt in her mind about her feelings for the ambassador and it was nice to know that Kelsey loved her and wanted her for a mother, but, unfortunately, he didn't feel the same.

When she thought back to the day that she had sent the guard away, it had seemed like he almost hated her. He certainly had been angry enough to fire her. In fact, if it hadn't been for Kelsey, he might have fired her on the spot. Bless the child; she had been willing to fight for what she wanted.

The more she thought about it, she became even more proud of Kelsey. She had come to teach the little girl, but the child had ended up teaching her something much more valuable. Kelsey wasn't afraid to speak up for what she wanted. Well, even if she didn't get it she knew what she wanted, and she was willing to take a step forward toward getting it.

She should be taking a life lesson from the five-year-old child. She should be willing to fight for what she wanted . . . and she wanted Trenton and Kelsey.

Her thoughts were interrupted when she heard someone walking through the woods. The person—or at least she hoped it was a person—was still a distance away, but she could hear leaves crunching. Her heart rate shot up, pounding against her ribs as she held the child tightly in front of her.

"Kelsey, get on the other side of the tree. Quick," she hissed. In the dark she felt around until she found a good-sized stick on the ground. If someone or something was coming after them, they were going to have to go through her to get to the child.

She weighed the stick in her hand, making slight hacking motions with it to determine how it felt in her hands. Yes, since she didn't have a gun, this would have to do.

She had braced her back against the tree as she closed her eyes and tried to make her mind blank so she could concentrate and listen.

"Kelsey! Natalie!"

Even though he was quite a distance away, both girls recognized the voice.

"Daddy!" Kelsey was around the tree and ahead of Natalie before she had even registered that the voice belonged to Trenton.

They both scrambled forward, pushing out through the limbs of the trees into a moonlit forest heavy with shadows. In the distance they could see a flashlight bobbing through the trees as Trenton rushed toward them.

"We're over here!" Natalie's aching body was forgotten with the prospect of seeing Trenton and going home.

"I'm coming!"

They were already moving toward his voice when they found each other.

"Daddy," she cried, reaching up her arms as he fell to his knees and cradled the child, the beam of the flashlight falling across Natalie and the stick in her hand. He registered the weapon she held but immediately turned his attention on Kelsey, kissing her several times between rubbing his hands over her hair and hugging her repeatedly.

"Oh, God, baby, I'm so glad to see you. I'm so glad you're okay," he said looking up into Natalie's face. "I'm glad to see both of you." When he aimed the flashlight on the stick in her hand she hesitated a moment, then tossed it to the ground and wiped her hands on her jeans.

She saw him smile before he redirected the light to the ground, casting them in shadows again.

"Of course, we're all right. We did exactly like you said. When we heard someone calling us we didn't answer because it wasn't you."

Natalie saw his smile, even in the dim moonlight. She didn't think he had ever looked better. Her eyes honed in on the bandage on the side of his head.

"What happened to you?"

"Just a small car accident," he said. "They insisted on checking me out at the hospital before they'd let me out to come get you two." He smiled again at Kelsey before trying to stand. Midway up, he hesitated a moment until he could put his right hand on his knee to help push himself up.

When he was standing straight, he held Kelsey tightly to his side, but he was looking at Natalie. The child's arms were wrapped around his legs like a tourniquet.

Natalie stared across into his eyes. In the shadows under the canopy of trees little moonlight was able to filter through, but even in the limited light from the flashlight currently pointing toward the ground, Trenton was able to see Natalie raise her eyebrows. He knew she'd be asking a lot of questions later.

"Natalie, I have a lot to thank you for. If you and Kelsey had been in the car . . ."

"Don't worry about that now . . ." She stopped midsentence, grabbing at Trenton's arm and jerking him forward when a shadow moved, materializing into a man. "Trenton!"

He saw her fear at the same time he felt her hand grab his arm. He jerked his head around to look behind him, relieved to immediately recognize the policeman.

"Oh, I'm sorry. I forgot that I brought the police with me," he said, turning back to Natalie, his eyes telling her how sorry he was to have frightened her.

"Sorry, I didn't mean to scare everyone," the policeman said, touching a couple fingers to the brim of his hat in a salute. "Everyone has been worried about you two. It's good to see you." He smiled in the dim light.

"We need to get you two back to the house," Trenton said. "I vote for hot chocolate," he suggested in an effort to lighten the mood.

"Yeah, me too. I'm cold," Kelsey announced, tucking herself even closer to her father. Trenton unbuttoned his shirt, wrapping it around the child's bare arms.

With the policeman in the lead and with only a tiny circle of flashlight to guide them, the group tromped through the woods. When they reached to the edge of the forest and stepped down onto the graveled road, Natalie stopped to look up toward the sky. A million stars twinkled in the dark canopy. It was a perfect evening that had almost become a nightmare. She sent a silent prayer heavenward to thank God that Trenton had not been badly hurt in the car wreck.

The policeman drove them back to the house where they were met with hugs from Mattie and Andrew.

No one was sleepy as they sat around the kitchen table talking about the excitement of the day. Clyde came in looking sheepish and hesitant.

"Trenton, I'm so sorry about hitting the Jeep. I had taken off after the guys when they left the house, but when I lost them in traffic I turned around and came back to see what needed to be done. I'm not sure which of us was over the line, but I'm so sorry." He appeared to be earnest, but Trenton wasn't sure. He would wait for the government to catch the guys and find out what the real story was. In the meantime, he was going to be very careful whom he trusted.

When the phone rang, everyone jumped, laughing nervously as Andrew answered.

"Lancaster residence," he told the caller.

"May I speak to Trenton? This is Special Agent Miller."

Andrew handed over the phone, whispering the name of the agent so Trenton would know who was calling.

"Yes, Doug. Do you have any news for me?"

"Good news, sir. We found the car and although it was stolen, we found a good print. We have a search warrant and we'll be on our way to, hopefully, get the guys in another fifteen or twenty minutes."

"Now, I don't want you to mention the warrant, but I want you to mention the fingerprints and see what kind of reaction you get from everyone there. Then call me back later at the number I left with your maid. All right?"

"Yeah. Great." Trenton hung up the phone. He paused a second before turning around with a huge smile on his face.

"Guess what? They found the car and even though it was stolen, they have fingerprints. Isn't that great?" He glanced around the crowd and everyone was smiling except Clyde.

"So does that mean that they've got the bad guys?"

"Well, Kelsey, as usual has asked the question that's on everyone's mind," laughed Andrew. The little girl smiled proudly as he patted her on the back.

"No, honey, it doesn't mean they've got the guys . . . yet, but it means they are on the trail of who they are," he smiled, glancing around at the people in the room.

"Well, I suggest we all go to bed and get some sleep," Trenton said, yawning.

"I agree." Natalie turned toward Kelsey, kneeling down and taking her small hands in her own. "Would you like to sleep over in my bed tonight?"

The child went from apprehensive to relieved in a matter of the two seconds it took for her to register the question and nod her head, a huge smile plastered across her face.

"Good. Come on. I want a bath and then sleep." She took Kelsey's hand and led her from the room, leaving the men to talk.

Trenton got Andrew's attention and gave a slight nod toward Clyde.

"Well, Clyde, come on, we need to get back on watch."

"Yeah. Mr. Lancaster, be careful. Check all the doors."

"Don't worry, I intend to be up the rest of the night. Since the front door is busted, I can't set the alarm."

"I'll watch the front if you want to get some sleep," Andrew offered.

"Okay, thanks."

Trenton knew he could trust Andrew, but he wasn't sure about Clyde. He hoped the FBI would find something soon.

Chapter Twelve

" . . . and Daddy, I wasn't even afraid. Honest. Miss Natalie kept telling me funny stories about when she was a little girl like me," she giggled before putting another bite of blueberry pancake in her mouth. "She was always getting into trouble," she said, looking over at Natalie.

"Okay, girlfriend, that's enough. Don't tell all my secrets," she told the child who was now laughing outright since she had gotten Natalie to respond.

"Well, I'm very proud of both of you. You were like undercover spies, hiding behind the lines in enemy territory," he told her seriously.

"Hum? I don't get it," she said, scrunching up her face.

"Never mind," he laughed.

"Are you planning to go into the office today?"

"No. I didn't get any sleep last night to speak of and I'm dead tired. I'll be staying home to rest."

When the doorbell rang, all three flinched. He knew it was going to take a while for them to settle down and get back to normal.

Andrew didn't even have a chance to tell Trenton who the caller was since Jennifer followed him into the dining room.

"My, my, don't we look like one cozy little family," she said with false brightness.

"May I please be excused?"

"Yes, honey. When I'm through here, we'll play a game together," he promised the child who was already slipping out the door.

"I think I'll take my coffee out on the patio so you two can have privacy to talk," Natalie said, standing to leave.

The door wasn't quite closed before Jennifer started talking.

"What's going on between you two?" She had stopped just inside the door of the dining room, but now she stalked forward, her eyes narrowed and her fist clinched around the strap of her shoulder purse.

Trenton turned stormy eyes on the woman standing over him, breathing fire like a dragon. "You know, I think I've had enough of your domineering ways. You're fired."

His voice didn't rise, nor did he frown. He simply made the statement in a level tone and turned his attention back to his pancake.

"What? You can't fire me. What would you do without me?"

"Yes, I can fire you, and I'll do quite nicely," he said, glancing up from his coffee.

"You mean you'd fire a loyal employee like myself and keep one who lies to you and puts your daughter in danger and has a thief for a brother?"

Trenton's hand stilled. He continued to stare at his food for a moment, gathering his thoughts before laying down the fork, standing and turning to face the woman who was now red in the face and fuming.

"What do you mean?"

"What do I mean?" Her mouth was hanging open as she frowned, taking a step back.

"How do you know what goes on here at the house?" When she didn't say anything, he asked another question.

"Who is giving you information on what goes on in my home?"

"No one," she said, taking another step backward as he took one forward.

"I'm only going to ask this question one more time, and then I'm calling the police if you don't answer or if I don't like your answer," he warned her, his hand snaking out to grab her arm.

"Ouch, you're hurting me," she whined, pulling against his hold.

"You don't know anything about hurting, but if you had anything to do with yesterday's break-in and putting my family at risk of harm, I'll show you hurting and I'll have no mercy," he hissed between his teeth, now leaning over her as she bent her head back to keep looking at him.

He waited a moment for emphasis, and then continued. "So, Jennifer, answer me right now and you have only one chance. Make your choice a good one," he suggested. "Who do you have giving you information about this household?" His fingers clamped a little tighter on her arm. He wanted to be sure she knew he meant what he was saying.

"Okay, okay. Don't get all in a dither," she laughed nervously. "I didn't mean any harm and I certainly didn't have anything to do with what happened yesterday.

"The truth is that I have a thing for you and," she pursed her lips in a pout before continuing. "I was a little jealous, I guess. I just wanted to know if you had fired her and what she was doing with dear little Kelsey. I wanted to be sure she was being a good tutor. After all, you did hire her on my recommendation. I felt responsible for the health and education of your daughter, so I had someone calling to let me know how she was doing with Kelsey."

"Who?"

"Oh, that doesn't matter since no harm was done, don't you agree?"

"No, I don't. I'm going to ask only one more time. Who was feeding you information about my family?"

"Oh," she pretended to shiver, "you make it sound so sinister. Okay, if you must know, it was Clyde. But he was doing it only to help me make you see that I was the best person for your career and your future and how Natalie doesn't care about Kelsey, she only cares about you. She wants you and she'll do anything to get you. She's a gold digger. She grew up poor and you are the answer to all her dreams," laughed the woman. She was growing more confident that she could make Trenton see things her way. After all, she knew how to control Trenton. He was like putty in her hands.

"Not that it's any of your business, but Natalie is the best thing that has happened to Kelsey since her mother died. In fact, she not only risked her life last night to keep my daughter safe, but when I found them last night she had a club in her hand and was ready to defend them. She had put herself between the danger and Kelsey and was ready to fight whoever had come after her."

Jennifer blinked a couple times, her mind racing for words to tear down the golden image he had of the tutor. "I see," she said, sighing. "She has apparently gotten to you. I see she has been able to convince you that she means well, but I can assure you that she is a liar and a thief."

"Oh, so now you're saying she stole something from me? It's not the brother now, but rather Natalie?"

"Well, I wasn't exactly accusing her. I just know that she would do anything not to lose her job."

"You're right about at least part of what you just said. I'm sure she would do anything . . . for Kelsey and myself. I just realized that, but thank goodness it isn't too late."

"Too late for what?"

"Too late to make things right and the first thing I'm doing toward that goal is to fire you."

He let go of her arm and put his hand in front of her, palm up. "Give me the keys to the company car and the office. Right now."

"No. You . . . no, I won't let you . . . you can't do that," she stuttered, horrified at what he had just said.

"I'm sure Andrew will drive you into town, and I'll have your personal things from the office packed and delivered to your home address. Keys?"

She was furious as she pulled out her keys and pulled the ones he wanted off the ring. "I drove my own car, but you'll be sorry."

"Good-bye."

After she had stormed from the house and screeched her tires leaving the estate, Trenton sighed. Thank goodness that was over.

He stood and walked outside to find Natalie standing across the yard, gazing down toward the lake. She turned and smiled when she heard him walking up.

His steps were slow and heavy as he stopped near her. He looked like the weight of the world was sitting on his shoulders. He stuck his hands in his pockets, putting most of his weight on his right leg.

"Are you all right?" She knew he was under a lot of stress right now, waiting for the government to find out who had been after him and Kelsey, but there seemed to be more than that.

"Normally I would lie and just say I'm fine. I'm tired of lying, so I'm going to tell you the truth. To answer your question, no, I'm not fine. First of all, I just fired Jennifer. She was acting like she owned me, and I recently discovered that I couldn't trust her. Besides that, I already know that she can't stand Kelsey."

"You mean she wanted you but not your daughter?"

"Yes, that's right. One day I went into her office to speak with her and she had stepped out. On her computer screen was a girl's boarding school in England. And to make it worse, have you noticed how Kelsey reacts whenever the woman comes around?"

"Yes," she told him, turning back to gaze toward the lake.

"I knew I had to get rid of her or find a way to keep her away from my daughter because Kelsey could sense that Jennifer didn't like her. Kids seem to have a sixth sense about things like that."

He took a casual step closer, his eyes never leaving Natalie's face. She was so beautiful, and never more beautiful than sporting the scratches across one cheek where some limbs had slashed across her face. She had risked her life to keep Kelsey safe and he would never forget it. He owed her more than he could ever repay. Without her, his daughter would have been in the car when it crashed. He shuddered to think about it.

There was so much more that he wanted to say to her, but he wasn't sure how she felt about him. She had always kept her distance with him, rarely relaxing when she was around him, so he wasn't sure how she'd react if he told her how he felt.

"Have you ever been to England?"

"No," she laughed, "I've never been out of the United States, but I'd love to travel. I think it would be exciting to see other cultures and architecture."

She watched him for a few moments as he gazed toward the horizon, before asking a question that had been on her mind.

"Do you miss England?"

He thought for a few moments before answering her question. "Sometimes. The weather is different here. Much milder," he smiled. "And it's cheaper to live, but sometimes I long to just be home and ride out across the fields behind my place. It's lovely there, especially this time of year. I think you'd like it."

"I'm sure I would. I love seeing and doing new things." After a moment she grinned. "Even learning to ride a horse."

"Ah, that. Are you angry with me for blackmailing you into learning to ride?"

She loved to see him relaxed and smiling. "No. Well, since we're being honest here, I'll have to say that I was a little angry that day, and maybe even the first couple days of lessons when I was so sore, but after that I actually got to like it. Clyde is a patient teacher, even if he is a hard taskmaster." She saw Trenton's expression close in. He was now frowning as he cleared his throat.

"Speaking about Clyde, tell me what you think of him personally."

"What do you mean? Are you asking if I trust him?"

"Not necessarily. I was mostly wondering about general observations or feelings, but you could start with trust. Do you trust him?"

She pondered her answer, not wanting to get Clyde in trouble if he wasn't in on the scheme to kidnap or kill Trenton, but since he asked she felt compelled to tell him her thoughts.

"When Kelsey and I were hiding, the first person to come looking for us was Clyde. I recognized his voice although I'm not sure that Kelsey did. Anyway, he wasn't that far from us and I wondered how he could have guessed so quickly that we might be in that area. It wasn't until an hour or more later that Andrew was hunting for us and he was a long way off. It sounded like he was just walking down the road and calling out."

"You're right, that sounds a little fishy."

"Maybe it's a coincidence."

"But maybe it's not. Listen, I want you to watch him for anything that he does or says that's different and I don't want you riding alone into the woods with him. I'm going to tell Andrew that I want someone else with you at all times when you ride. I'll tell Clyde that it's because if the guys show back up he'd need help to protect you two."

"Trenton, does anyone else know about the tunnel?"

"Only Andrew, why?"

"Well, I thought that you could put a couple flashlights in there and maybe some food and water and then if there was ever a problem, I could take Kelsey and hide in there. That way you'd know where we are and wouldn't have to worry about us trying to get away from the house."

"You wouldn't be afraid in there alone with Kelsey?"

"Not as long as I had a flashlight."

"Good enough. That's a grand plan you've come up with. That will take a lot off my mind. You'll need to know the code to get in the tunnel. It's S-A-F-E-T-Y. Actually it's the numbers that correspond to those letters on the phone dial. So the code is 7-2-3-3-8-9."

She took a moment to say the numbers aloud a couple times. "I won't forget it," she smiled. "But if I do, I won't forget S-A-F-E-T-Y. That's very ingenious." She repeated the series of numbers several times in her head, committing them to memory in case she ever needed to use the tunnel.

"I'll take care of getting the things into the tunnel today. There's vents, so you don't have to worry about running out of oxygen."

"Okay. Well, we'd better be getting back. Miss Kelsey will be worried about us if we take too long."

Trenton turned with her and started back, but what he really wanted to do was tell her just how he felt. He wanted her in his arms. He wanted her kissing him and loving him. He wanted, he wanted, he wanted. He wanted something that he couldn't have. He hadn't been looking for love, but it had snuck up behind him. Besides, he would be the worst kind of man to make a pass at his child's nanny.

His heart was aching. Inside he felt disappointment building up to block his throat and choke him. Sometimes life wasn't fair. He had never expected to find another woman who would be able to steal his heart, but this young woman had slipped under his radar and placed a noose around his neck. He was hers, but she didn't even know it. She didn't know her power.

He knew if he told her how he felt and if it made her uncomfortable she'd probably leave, and then he and Kelsey would be alone again. Kelsey would lose the best teacher and best friend she had ever had.

No, he couldn't take the chance. He had to keep his feelings to himself.

At the window above, a little girl stood looking down at her two most favorite people in the world. She loved them both and she wished they could love each other and get married. She wanted them to kiss. That's what people in love did, but they hadn't kissed. In fact, they hadn't even touched.

As they neared the house, she stepped away from the window and sighed. This was just another thing that she wanted that she wouldn't get to have. She wiped her hand angrily across her face to get rid of the tears that she hated. Only babies cried.

Chapter Thirteen

Trenton took a nap, but by afternoon he was up and ready to go ride horses.

"Yeah! Miss Natalie," Kelsey called, running toward the living room where her tutor was sitting reading. "Daddy said he will go riding with us. Come on," she said, tugging on Natalie's hand. "Get dressed so we can go riding. Chester has missed me," she announced.

Natalie couldn't help but respond to the child's enthusiasm. "Okay, lead the way," she laughed, laying her book on the sofa.

When Kelsey was at the top of the stairs, she stopped. "Come on. Hurry so he won't change his mind."

"He won't change his mind," she chuckled. She couldn't believe how carefree she felt knowing that she would get to spend the next couple hours with the two people she loved.

She had been giving it a lot of thought and since she had decided to fight for what she wanted, she hadn't made any move to convince Trenton that he couldn't live without her. She was going to have to come up with a plan.

It was late afternoon by the time they all were dressed and had gotten the horses saddled. They rode for almost an hour before dinner, hunger making them all willing to turn around and head back to the stable.

Clyde came out smiling as he congratulated Kelsey on how good her form was on Chester. Taking the reins, he led the horses inside to be brushed, watered, and fed while the three walked up the path toward the house.

Natalie turned in a circle as they were walking. She was so overcome with the beauty of the land that tears came into her eyes.

"What's the matter?" Trenton asked.

"It's just so pretty here. Look out there," she told them. "See all the different types of trees and all the shades of green?"

"Yeah, it's pretty remarkable, isn't it?"

"Mr. Lancaster!"

Trenton turned toward the porch where Mattie was standing, holding the phone above her head. "There is an agent on the phone for you," she called out.

"Kelsey and I will go up and change and meet you downstairs for dinner in a little while, okay?"

"Yeah, that sounds good." He headed toward his office, shutting the door quietly behind him before lifting the phone.

"Trenton here."

"Mr. Lancaster, this is Special Agent Miller. I need you to go down to the police station, please."

"Why?"

"There's been a murder and I need you to identify the murder weapon."

"What? You think I killed someone?" His heart thudded against his rib cage as the very thought of being accused of murder and being arrested slammed into him.

"No, I'm sorry to have upset you. We know who did the killing. We have the person on a security surveillance tape. The reason we need you is that the murder weapon appears to be the knife from your collection that you reported stolen."

Trenton was speechless. He had a queasy feeling in his stomach just thinking about his knife being used in such a manner. Who had stolen the knife and then killed someone with it? This whole mess was getting out of hand. He wasn't even sure he wanted the knife back in his house.

"Yes, yes, of course. I'll come down right away. What's the address?"

"I gave it to your maid when she thought you weren't home yet. We'd appreciate you coming just as soon as possible. We'd like to close this case quietly and quickly. We're also going to try to keep your name out of the papers. No one really needs to know where the murder weapon came from. When you get to the station, asked for Sergeant McKinney."

"Yeah, sure. I'll come down right now and get it over with. Bye."

Trenton punched in the number down at the stable.

"Clyde, I need to go into town. Could you bring the car around?"

He sank into the chair behind his desk, staring into space. Life had been upside down the last few weeks. What next? There were days he longed to be back in England and away from all that his job in America had exposed him to. He wanted to be on the farm where he could see the animals and the countryside. But Natalie was here, as well as the chance to make a difference in the world by being on UN committees.

When he heard the car drive up in front of the house he left the office, stopping in the kitchen to get the address from Mattie.

"Will you please tell Natalie and Kelsey that I have to go to the police station and should be back within two hours? Tell them not to wait on dinner. I'll grab something when I get back."

"Yes, sir."

All the way to the police station his mind swirled. *Who had used the knife? And who was dead? That was stupid*, he thought. *I didn't even think to ask.*

"Sir, I know where we're going, but are you at liberty to tell me why we're heading to the police station?"

"I don't know if I can say yet. I'll let you know if I can," he promised.

The station was swarming with people, several languages being spoken while he waited behind a woman holding a tiny boy. The oversized room was bustling with hurt or frightened people; it was filled with people needing help.

"Thank goodness I'm just here to identify my knife," he muttered to himself, stepping forward as the lady in front of him was shuffled off to a desk to speak with an officer.

"May I help you?"

"I'm supposed to ask for Sergeant McKinney."

"Just a moment." The officer punched in three numbers and waited until someone answered on the other end of the phone. "There's someone here asking for you." He hung up the phone. "You can wait over to the left," he pointed.

"Next?"

Trenton stood out of the way, watching the milling crowd. Every category was represented from young to old and from rich to poor. There were men in business suits and street women in short, tight skirts and halter tops. This was what he was used to in England. The masses.

Within a couple minutes, he saw an officer make his way toward the desk, ask a question, and be directed toward him.

"Good afternoon. I'm Detective McKinney. Are you Ambassador Lancaster?"

"Yes, but Trenton, please. I understand my knife was used in a murder?"

"It appears so, but that's why we asked you to come in and identify your knife. All we had was the picture you supplied with the theft report, and even though it's very unique, we need a positive first-hand identification. Come with me," he said, starting to walk toward the back of the room, weaving in and out between people.

"I didn't think to ask who was killed. Is that something that you can tell me?"

"I don't see why not since it'll be in the evening paper. The victim was found in her apartment and had been dead for about four to six hours. Her name was Jennifer Greene."

The officer kept walking, but Trenton stopped in his tracks. The confused noise of a hundred voices arguing and yelling and crying was suddenly a distant roar, like the sounds were trying to reach him through a pool of water. As the ringing in his ears increased, the room's noise gradually faded to a resonating hum—a hum that drew his attention inward to focus on the dimming light before his eyes.

He felt weak, his arms hanging limp at his sides, his muscles nonreactive as he opened his mouth, but no words formed. As the momentary confusion began to pass, he felt a chill raise bumps on his arms. Why did they keep the room so cold?

"Are you all right?" Someone had taken hold of his arm and was talking to him, but the sound was reedy and far away.

The confusion now passed quickly, leaving him feeling embarrassed at his weakness.

"I'm sorry. I'm all right," he assured the officer.

A woman bumped into him and kept walking without saying anything, but he hardly noticed. He brought his eyes back to the officer. "Are you sure it was Jennifer?"

"Yes, quite sure. There has already been a positive identification by a family member. You knew the deceased?"

"Yes, she was my social secretary." He didn't figure it was necessary to tell the policeman that he had fired her just before she was killed. "In fact, she was at my house this morning. She left about eight o'clock."

"Were there witnesses to her being there and her leaving?"

"I would imagine so. My five-year-old daughter, her nanny, the cook, the estate manager, and the stable hands were all there."

"Can you prove where you were between eight o'clock and now?"

"Yes. I was with my daughter and her nanny playing games and eating until the call came to come here."

"Okay. I'm sure they'll need a statement, but that should clear you of any involvement. That will also help them with the timeline. After we're finished I'll put you in touch with the officer heading up the investigation."

When they reached the Property Room, Detective McKinney requested the murder weapon, allowing Trenton to view it.

It didn't take but a glance to determine that it was his knife. At least he now knew who had stolen from him. Had she been trying to get Natalie in trouble by implying her family had been involved in the theft? Whatever the reason, it didn't matter now.

"Yes, it's my knife," he heaved a sigh as he turned his back on the counter.

"You know, Ambassador, I don't know why your secretary was killed, but chances are good that she'd have been killed with something else if the knife hadn't been available. Please don't feel guilty," suggested the policeman, handing the knife back to the property clerk.

"No, I won't. I was just thinking about all the high hopes she had for the future," he said, stretching out his hand to shake with the officer.

It was a quiet ride back to the estate. All he wanted to do was wrap his arms around Kelsey and Natalie. He wanted to keep them close and not let anything happen to them, but now they needed to be more careful than ever. The men who had come on the estate and broken into the house hadn't been identified yet, but if the two incidents were related, the men had no problem with killing someone.

When he walked through the front door, Natalie was waiting for him.

"I just heard about Jennifer on the news. I'm so sorry," she said, reaching out to touch his arm.

He gently took her upper arms in his hands and pulled her forward. Her skin was warm and soft as she slid her arms around his waist and he snuggled her close. His hands slid up into her silky hair to draw her head down to his chest where he held her near his aching heart, holding her like fragile china, too precious to risk breaking.

With his cheek laid against the top of her head, he felt the moment that she relaxed, her body curving into his, meshing with him to bond into one unit. Her unique fragrance of musky herbal shampoo intoxicated him as it soothed his senses and calmed his nerves. His eyes closed as he drew strength from her closeness and warmth. He never wanted to let her go. She fit perfectly. As he rubbed his hands up and down her back, she sighed, allowing her eyes to drift closed on a slow, low moan.

He could have this every day if only she was interested in him. If only she loved him like she loved Kelsey. Oh, he knew she was lending him strength and comfort right now, but that wasn't enough. It wouldn't be enough until she had his ring on her finger and was tucked snuggly in his bed with him every night. But was he being selfish?

They held each other and rocked for quite awhile until she pulled back to look up into his face. "How did she die? All the television said was that she had been found dead."

"She was stabbed . . . with the knife from my collection," he replied, releasing her and turning toward the living room. He stopped a few feet away. "I guess she was the one who stole it." Without her warmth he felt adrift, lonely, lost. He needed her more than he had realized, more than he wanted to admit.

"Or whomever stole it went to her house with it and killed her," she said, frowning. "Do they have any clues as to who did it?"

"Yes and no. It happened sometime after she left here. Thank goodness I was with you and Kelsey the entire day or I might be a suspect, especially if they find out I had just fired her. But he mentioned something about someone being on the surveillance camera."

"Who would want her dead?"

"I wish I knew. Regardless of her faults, she didn't deserve to die." He closed his eyes for a moment, taking a deep breath and releasing it slowly. "Right now the biggest thing I'm concerned about is if it's in any way related to the men who broke in here the other night. If so, they have no compunction against killing and that makes them very dangerous." He ran his blunt fingers through his hair, leaving rows furrowed across the top.

"I don't think I'll tell Kelsey."

"She already knows. She was sitting right beside me when the bulletin interrupted the show we were watching. They showed a picture of her with you, so there wasn't much chance that she wouldn't notice."

"Was she upset?"

"Not in the least. She said that sometimes bad people

die, but that she didn't think Jennifer was going to heaven to be with Jesus," she smiled as she relayed the conversation.

"She could be right."

She could tell he was hurting. *Fight for what you want.* She hesitated only a moment longer before stepping up to his back and wrapping her arms around his waist, resting her cheek on his back for a moment before pulling away. "Why don't you come out to the kitchen? There's a plate of food in the oven, and I'll pour you a cup of coffee."

"Honey, you've got a deal," he said, turning to face her before wrapping his arm around her waist and walking beside her toward the kitchen.

Natalie's heart was breaking. He was holding her because of his grief about the woman he had cared about. He was holding her now only because he needed a warm body to cling to. Tomorrow he'd be sorry and he'd go back to being silent again. How much longer could she stand loving him and not being loved in return?

Her heart was breaking, but he only saw her as the nanny. To him she was only the woman who taught Kelsey. That was all. How long could she continue to live in the same house, sit at his table, share meals and watch him and Kelsey together? How long could she stay here under these conditions?

She was quiet as she served his dinner, filled his coffee cup, and excused herself to go check on Kelsey.

* * *

The three were quiet the next morning at the breakfast table. Even Kelsey was content to eat her oatmeal without a lot of chatter.

Natalie had slept very little and if Trenton's repeated yawns meant anything, neither had he.

"Are you going into the office this morning?"

"Not until later. I have some work that I can do from home and I don't have any meetings today. I can probably get more done here since the office will be buzzing all day with the latest news."

There was no need to mention Jennifer's name. It was still headlining every newscast and her picture was smiling up from the front page of the newspaper. Natalie could well understand that everyone would be discussing something that had hit so close to home.

"I'll be busy today with Kelsey's riding lesson and then her school lessons, so it should be relatively quiet for you," she said, setting down her fork after only eating half of what was on her plate.

Trenton had just finished eating and had pushed his coffee cup back when the front door chimes rang through the house.

Kelsey glanced up, but returned to making grooves in the mountain of oatmeal. Trenton was surprised when Mattie came to the dining room door.

"Sir, an Agent Miller is here to speak with you. I've shown him into your office."

"Excellent. I'll see him right away," he said, standing and placing his napkin on the table.

"We'll take our riding lesson and then we'll be in the workroom upstairs if you need us," Natalie said, momentarily reaching out to touch his hand before quickly drawing it back and stuffing it in her lap.

He appreciated her offer of support, but he wanted to keep this mess as far from her and Kelsey as possible. He reached out to gently touch the underside of her chin with the tips of his fingers as she sat looking up at him. After a brief smile, he turned and headed toward his office.

He dreaded this meeting. On one hand he hated the thought of talking about Jennifer's death, but he knew it was inevitable. He strode into the office with his hand outstretched.

"Good morning. Can I get you some coffee before we start?"

"Good morning, Mr. Lancaster. No, thank you. I've already had my quota of coffee for the day and it's not even ten o'clock," he smiled as he shook hands with Trenton.

"So, what can I do for you?"

"Nothing really. I just wanted to give you an update."

"Did you find Jennifer's killer?"

"Yes and no." When Trenton raised his eyebrows at the vague answer, the agent smiled. "First, let me give you a little background. It'll help you understand. Your groom, Clyde, is a retired FBI agent." He smiled again when Trenton's eyes opened wider. "He was a foreign agent who has been retired for about ten or twelve years.

After retirement he took a job working with horses, which was his hobby and second love. He was living on this estate, taking care of the Michaels' horses when we got suspicious about Harry Michaels and some overseas agents from Europe. So, we asked Clyde to come out of retirement long enough to help us with this one case. It was all very classified, so you were never told."

"So you arrested this Michaels character?"

"Yeah, but we knew he had some help and we've been working to trace those people. Seems one of the front line was your secretary, Jennifer. We know who killed her . . . got him on surveillance camera arriving at her apartment building and leaving less than fifteen minutes later. Maybe what I should say is he was running from her place. We tracked him to a flight back to France. We'll get him soon."

"So what about the guys who stormed into my home?"

"We got one of them and he named the others in a bargaining agreement. They're really small-time hired guns. They were supposed to deliver you to our fugitive, unharmed, so we believe he wanted to use your daughter as leverage to guarantee you voted as they wanted."

Trenton rubbed his hand down his face. He shuddered at the thought of thugs holding Kelsey and forcing his vote in order to try to get her back. "Thank you, God," he whispered.

"So, that's about it. We won't quit until we find them and, in the meantime, we're asking you to be extra careful."

"You can bet I will. Thank you very much," he said, standing and stretching out his hand.

"You bet. I think you have a couple great assets with Clyde and your driver, Andrew Drummond. He has quite a reputation in Britain at Scotland Yard. And you can't do better than Clyde." He shook Trenton's hand and headed for the front door.

"Thank you, sir. I can't thank you enough for all you're doing for my family."

That night they ate out on the patio to celebrate the police getting the "bad guys." As Natalie watched father and daughter laughing and sharing fruited margaritas, her heart ached. She felt like she was on the outside looking in on a relationship she had no right to be a part of. She felt empty. She was with two people whom she loved, but she was alone. She envied their loving relationship.

"I've got a headache," she said, standing and putting her hand to her forehead. "I'm going to go up and lie down for awhile." She couldn't get away fast enough.

She was almost to the top of the stairs when the first tears fell, but she was safely behind her closed door before sinking onto her bed and holding a pillow close to muffle her sobs.

Kelsey had told her daddy she would play in her room for an hour until time for bed, but it was no fun alone. She crept down the hall to Miss Natalie's room and stood listening to see if she could hear anything. She hoped her teacher was awake so she could go in and talk with her. Maybe she could get her to help put together the new dollhouse her daddy had brought home.

When she got to the door and raised her hand to knock, she heard what sounded like Miss Natalie crying. Did grown-ups cry like that? It sounded like in the movies when someone had died and all the women were crying at the funeral. Was Miss Natalie crying because Miss Jennifer died and she would now have to go to a funeral?

She wasn't sure what to do. Whenever she cried, Miss Natalie would hold her and tell her everything was all right. Is that what you did when grown-ups cried? Maybe she'd better ask her daddy.

She turned from the door and ran down the hallway to the stairs. Looking around quickly, she held onto the banister post, stood on her tiptoes, and swung a leg over the banister to quickly slide down to the bottom. When her butt ran into the newel post, she slid off and ran down the hall toward her father's office.

She had just rounded the corner into the office when she plowed into someone standing near the bookcase.

"Daddy!" she said, throwing her arms around his legs and holding on tight. I need you," she said, frowning up at him as he leaned down to swing her up into his arms, planting a loud kiss on her cheek.

"Did you yell at Miss Natalie?"

He pulled back to look at her. "What? What makes

you think I yelled at Miss Natalie?" He sat down in the nearest chair, sitting her on his lap and jiggling his legs to bounce her up and down.

"She's up in her room crying. And I don't think it's because Miss Jennifer has been killed," she concluded. "Miss Jennifer was never nice to her."

"Well, don't worry about Miss Natalie, honey. Maybe she had a rough day or is just tired. I'll check on her later, okay?" He leaned in to kiss his daughter's forehead.

"Daddy? Why don't you marry Miss Natalie and have babies and we can all live happily ever after like in my books?"

He was stunned and speechless. He had no idea his daughter was thinking along these lines. How do you tell a five-year-old that you'd love to marry her teacher, but you can't because even though your daddy loves the teacher, the teacher doesn't love your daddy? And never again would he get himself into a one-sided love match. He swam through those shark-infested waters before and had been miserable. He didn't ever want to do that again.

"But she's not happy. Can you make her happy again?" Big eyes looked to him to fix whatever was wrong, but he didn't know how to fix Natalie's problem, whatever it was.

"I'll see what I can do," he promised, hoping to avoid any more discussion.

"Now?"

He hesitated for only a moment before he realized

that what she was asking him to do was exactly what he wanted to be doing. He didn't want to sit down here knowing she was crying upstairs.

"Okay, Munchkin. I'll give you a ride upstairs, and then I want you to go in and play with your dolls for a bit while I talk with Miss Natalie. When I'm finished, I'll come in to your room and read you a story. Deal?"

"Deal," she said, all smiles now that she had her father's promise to fix things.

"Here," he said, lifting her off his lap and turning around with her in his arms. "Stand on the chair." When he turned his back toward her, she latched her tiny arms around his neck and held on as his strong arms came around to wrap around her legs to support her.

"Gettie up," she yelled.

He took off at a loping gallop, bouncing her along like a rag doll as he stomped up the stairs, down the hall, and into her room to drop her backwards onto the bed. Her giggles filled the room as she bounced a couple times and came to rest with him hovering over her prone body.

"I love you, Munchkin."

"I love you too, Daddy." In a loud whisper she added her instructions. "Now go make Miss Natalie not cry so she can be happy."

"Yes, ma'am, I'll try my best. I'll be back soon. Get into your nightgown for me." He kissed her nose and tickled her ribs before standing and heading out the door.

He shut Kelsey's door and stood in the hallway wondering how he had gotten himself into this mess. He didn't know what to say to a woman who was crying. He preferred to go the other way when a woman got weepy. He allowed a soft moan to escape before admitting defeat and heading toward her room. Procrastinating wasn't a good option, so he might as well take his medicine like a man. Besides, he had no clue why she was crying, but he sure hoped it wasn't his fault.

He stepped up to her door, raised his hand to knock and then hesitated, listening for a moment before tapping lightly.

"Just a minute," she called out.

She had given in and cried, but as usual all she gained from it was red, puffy eyes and a headache. She lay on the bed with her eyes closed, thinking about what life had been like prior to coming to work for Trenton and wondering if she was willing to leave and go back to West Virginia. Could she stand to leave the child whom she had fallen in love with? Could she leave Trenton? *Oh, man, life just wasn't fair,* she thought, covering her eyes with her hand. She had been dealt a rotten hand, but she didn't think she could fold and walk away. She was going to have to play out the hand. She didn't think she could win, she hoped she wouldn't lose, so it looked like the best she could hope for would be to break even. She hoped Lady Luck would smile on her.

When the light knock came at the door, she flinched. It was probably Kelsey and she'd be upset at seeing her teacher had been crying. There was nothing else to do except tell Kelsey she had a headache. At least that was the truth.

She slid her legs over the edge of the bed and stood to walk slowly to the door, dragging her feet like an inmate walking that final mile. When she had opened the door a few inches, she was stunned to see Trenton standing on the threshold.

"Oh, did you want something?" She lowered her eyes, hoping to hide her puffy, red eyes. She prayed her face wasn't blotchy like it got sometimes when she cried.

"Can I come in?"

Oh Lord, why did he pick now to want to talk? "Sure, come on in. I was just lying down. I have a headache," she told him softly, turning her back on him to walk back toward her desk.

"Small wonder when you've been crying," he said matter-of-factly, stepping into the room and quietly shutting the door.

She was stunned. Although his words had stopped her in the middle of the room, she didn't turn around. She was horrified that he was in her bedroom and horrified that he knew she had been crying. She had hoped to pass off her red eyes to the effects of a migraine. "What makes you say that?"

"Kelsey came down to tell me and asked me to come make it all better," he smiled slightly. He was trying to gauge if he was making it better or worse, but with her back to him he was only able to guess. What did a bowed head and slumped shoulders mean?

She could feel her face getting hot. Without thinking, she turned to face him, her eyes growing larger in surprise and despair. "Oh no, I didn't think she'd be able to hear."

He saw the moment she realized and started to turn away. His arms shot out to stop her, tugging gently to draw her near. She hung her head, angry with herself for upsetting the child.

"I'll go talk to her and let her know I'm fine," she said, trying to step back out of his reach.

"I don't think that's a good idea at the moment. You're eyes are red and swollen and you could try to tell her that you're fine, but I don't think she'd believe you." His words, spoken softly as to a frightened child, halted her retreat.

He ran his finger gently under her eyes, tracing the dark smudges. Even with puffy eyes and light red blotches on her face, she was beautiful. He would never tire of looking at her and seeing her so upset made his heart ache.

"What's wrong?" His voice had lowered and his hands were gentle as he pulled her closer and loosely wrapped his arms around her.

At first her body was stiff, resisting his offered comfort, but his aura of strength wrapped around her, overloading her senses, satisfying her desire to be loved and cherished. His deep voice soothed the raw and bleeding heart, a heart aching for what she wanted, but what was so far out of her reach. It was no use fighting her feelings any longer.

As she relaxed, he pulled her closer, his shirt soaking up her renewed tears as she laid her head on his shoulder and allowed her tears to flow.

"Shhh, it'll be okay," he promised. His hand stroked her hair like she had seen him do to Kelsey while her arms hesitated, poised to wrap around his waist when he pulled back a couple inches and leaned down to place butterfly kisses on her lips.

She opened her eyes to see emotion shining from his eyes. Was it love? Was he feeling sorry for her? She didn't want his pity.

"I know these tears aren't because of Jennifer. Kelsey just told me that Jennifer wasn't very nice to you."

She couldn't stop the nervous little laugh that slipped out. "She has told you quite a bit today. Did she say anything else?" Natalie pulled back from his arms to wipe the tears from under her eyes.

"No, not directly. Do you know that she loves you?"

"Yes," she nodded, "and that concerns me a bit. I can't stay forever and she'll experience another loss when I leave."

"Hummm. I have only a couple questions to that last statement." He put his finger under her chin and gently lifted until her eyes rose to meet his.

"I'm wondering why you can't stay forever and were you planning on going away any time soon?"

His stare penetrated to her heart, stabbing it and making it bleed. Why couldn't she stay forever? She'd like nothing better, but he didn't love her and that was the only way she could stay. Oh, sure, he was concerned about her, but then he was concerned about everyone who lived in the house and worked for him.

She continued to stare into his eyes without being able to speak. "Cat got your tongue? Speaking of which, I thought it might be a nice gift for Kelsey for her birthday."

She frowned, unable to follow his conversation.

"A kitten. I was thinking Kelsey would love to have a kitten," he chuckled.

"Oh." She tried to step back, but he refused to allow her to run away without answering his question. She released a breath that had been pressing against her aching lungs. "I think a kitten would be fine."

"Now, you answered that, so why not answer my first two questions?"

This was really putting her on the spot. What should she say? What *could* she say? "I don't know what to say." When he remained silent, staring as if waiting for her to continue, she swallowed and licked her suddenly dry lips.

"I can't stay here forever because Kelsey won't need me forever and no, I wasn't planning on leaving . . . at least not right away."

"Do you ever want to leave?" His voice had gotten deeper and softer. He was almost whispering as he continued to keep her chin lifted with his finger.

Her eyes closed, shutting out the face that haunted her dreams and sent her heart rate into overdrive just by walking into the room. She didn't want to look at him and try to guess what he was thinking. This was too difficult. She didn't know how to answer him without confessing her love, so it would be better if she just kept her mouth closed.

"Natalie, please answer this next question honestly." He hesitated only a moment before continuing. "I know you love Kelsey, I can see it on your face when you look at her and hear it in your voice when you talk to her. What I need to know is if you think you could ever care for me," he said, closing his eyes for a moment as if in prayer before opening them to stare into the dark pools that widened as they filled with tears.

"Yes," she whispered. "I care about you already."

"Do you love me?"

Be willing to fight for what you want. Without hesitation, her face relaxed, a soft smile creeping across her face as her eyes brightened. "Yes."

That was all he needed to hear. Before she could take her next breath, he had wrapped his arms around her and was twirling her around in a circle, his head thrown back and a deep rumbling laugh booming into the room.

When he sat her feet back on the floor, he glanced over her shoulder to see Kelsey peeking in the door.

"Come on in, Munchkin," he said, smiling down at his daughter who ran into the room and threw her small arms around both their legs.

"So Miss Natalie isn't upset anymore?"

"No, I'm not. In fact, your daddy has made me very happy."

"Good. Usually he has to kiss me to make me feel happy again." Her smile was sly, but neither adult cared.

"I didn't make all the right decisions the first time around, so things weren't as good as they could have been, but if you're willing to trust me, I vow to work hard at making my two girls very happy. Do you think I'm worth taking a risk on?"

"Oh yes. If you think you can handle being married to someone from the hills of West Virginia, I think I can handle an ambassador from England."

"Well, it might surprise you to know about the simple background I came from. We're not so very different. But we've got all the time in the world to talk about that and get to know that side of each other."

"Okay, but you forgot the kiss that's supposed to make me feel better," she reminded him, glancing down at Kelsey who was all smiles.

"Not for long," he said softly as he leaned closer, lifting his hands to cradle her face and draw it in to his masterful lips. The soft moan told him that he had reached her soul.

Beside them, Kelsey clasped her hands together. She was going to have a new mommy.